'How many  you?' cried K

'I'm quite happy as I am.'

'You're a coward,' Max said contemptuously. 'You're so afraid to fall that you won't climb an inch.' He looked down into her upturned face with a menacing smile. 'Cowards have to learn that it's easier to fight than to run away because no matter how fast you run fate can run faster.'

Dear Reader

For many of us, this is the best period of the year—the season of goodwill and celebration—though it can make big demands on your time and pocket, too! Or maybe you prefer to spend these mid-winter months more quietly? Whatever you've got planned, Mills & Boon's romances are always there for you as special friends at the turn of the year: easy, entertaining and comforting reads that are great value for money. Stay warm, won't you!

The Editor

Charlotte Lamb was born in London in time for World War II, and spent most of the war moving from relative to relative to escape bombing. Educated at a convent, she married a journalist, and now has five children. The family lives in the Isle of Man. Charlotte Lamb has written over a hundred books, most of them for Mills & Boon.

FESTIVAL SUMMER

BY

CHARLOTTE LAMB

MILLS & BOON LIMITED
ETON HOUSE, 18-24 PARADISE ROAD
RICHMOND, SURREY TW9 1SR

All the characters in this book have no existence outside the imagination of the Author, and have no relation whatsoever to anyone bearing the same name or names. They are not even distantly inspired by any individual known or unknown to the Author, and all the incidents are pure invention.

All rights reserved. The text of this publication or any part thereof may not be reproduced or transmitted in any form or by any means, electronic or mechanical, including photocopying, recording, storage in an information retrieval system, or other-wise, without the written permission of the publisher.

This book is sold subject to the condition that it shall not, by way of trade or otherwise, be lent, resold, hired out or otherwise circulated without the prior consent of the publisher in any form of binding or cover other than that in which it is published and without a similar condition including this condition being imposed on the subsequent purchaser.

First published in Great Britain in 1977 by Mills & Boon Limited

© Charlotte Lamb 1977

*Australian copyright 1977
Philippine copyright 1993
This edition 1993*

ISBN 0 263 77916 5

01-9301

Made and printed in Great Britain

CHAPTER ONE

THE Press were fond of referring to them as 'The Magnificent Milfords' and, on occasions like this, thought the youngest member of the family, the title was not inapt. They were all grouped around the grand piano at this moment, half-consciously posing under the battery of eyes, as dazzling as the chandelier which hung above their heads.

She was the only member of her illustrious family who had not gone on the stage—the shy one, the daughter few people knew about, with her fine-boned little face, straight dark hair and retiring manner. Once she had said wistfully to Sebby, 'I'm as out of place among the others as a pussy cat among lions...'

'We're all what God made us,' Sebby had said unanswerably, offering her no comfort.

She stood alone, in a corner, unnoticed by the throng of guests whose eyes were all fixed in fascination upon her family. Viola was singing a witty little song from the revue in which she was currently appearing. Her hair, like blonde feathers, lay elegantly across her pale forehead. Viola's latest affectation was to wear no make-up—since her skin had a transparent pallor which was most enchanting she could afford to do so. Her slanting green eyes slid sideways, wicked and funny, teasing the man who was playing the piano for her.

Cleo, on the other hand, was looking sulky. She hated to have the limelight switched away from herself to her sister. Cleo was, as she was well aware, the most dazzling of the three girls—as sinuous as a tigress, with a shining golden tan and a curved figure, her red-gold hair a silken curtain worn loose or, on rare occasions, swept up into an elegant chignon. Sometimes, looking at her, Katrine wondered if she had dreamt it, invented her far-off childhood, when Cleo had been a tomboy with ginger hair and freckles who let her trail along on fishing expeditions to the river which ran behind their London home. Certainly nobody now would believe it. Cleo Milford was one of the new sex symbols of the age. Her face and body writhed in supple beauty across magazine covers, billboards and television advertisements. Anyone less likely to have had ginger hair and freckles could not be imagined. Katrine, with a smothered giggle, wondered what Cleo would do if, one day, she dropped a hint to some gossip columnist. She wouldn't do it, of course—for one thing family loyalty forbade it, for another Cleo could be a most alarming enemy, and finally Katrine still cherished the memory of her tomboy sister and her own fondness for Cleo kept that old memory shut away in the privacy of her head.

Cass, her brother, was much as he had always been, even at the earliest age she could remember— when he was a lordly, scornful schoolboy of twelve and she was toddling up and down in his wake imploring him to let her join his game of cricket. He had been a very adult schoolboy, one of those who always look immaculate in blazer and cap, his grey eyes coolly self-contained.

There was never any question as to his future career. Cass always knew what he wanted, and how to get it. He had had a brilliant meteoric rise—a small but dazzling part in his first West End play putting him at once into the category of actors everyone remembers. Katrine often wondered if Cass was happy. He was so shuttered, so withdrawn. What did he think, behind that almost too handsome face, and what did he want out of life apart from success?

Viola had finished her song. Everyone clapped and laughed. Rolf Milford, their father, kissed Viola elegantly, looking proud and yet modest in some indefinable way. He was aware that his children were an extension of himself and his very real affection for them was complicated by his professional attitude. Katrine watched him wistfully. She knew he felt her to be a failure, the changeling of the family. Her shyness and lack of ambition baffled and irritated Rolf. Katrine tried to make up for it by self-effacing eagerness to help. She waited on him hand and foot when he was at home, took great pains with meals for him, acted as his secretary if the need arose and was, unfailingly, saddened by a feeling of inadequacy.

Rolf was fond of throwing extravagant parties.

Tonight the occasion he celebrated was the last night of a successful run in a modern black comedy of scarifying intensity, a new departure for him. He had, she knew, been nervous when he accepted the part. In the event, it had been a box office success, to his relief.

'I only hope I haven't scared away my real public,' he had said uneasily to Sebby once.

'You can do no wrong where they're concerned,' Sebby had assured him cheerfully.

Among the guests tonight were a number of journalists. Katrine could see Roddy Sumner, in a black velvet suit and a shirt with a lace jabot, telling Cleo a wildly embellished story about a certain eminent American film star. Katrine had heard the tale before. It was common knowledge among their friends, but Cleo was pretending she had never heard it, if her expression of wide-eyed amusement was anything to go by. The poor man, under domestic pressure, had got uncharacteristically drunk at a Los Angeles restaurant and ended up singing opera in a neon-lit fountain under the eyes of an excited crowd while photographers jostled to snatch shots of him from every angle.

'Poor old Piers,' her father murmured, joining her. 'He lets his hair down just once in twenty years, and the whole world is agog! Why do people love to see stars like Piers tumbled from their pedestals?'

'Human nature,' she said regretfully, keeping a weather eye on the bar. Journalists drank so much more than one ever expected, and she was sure she could see a look of wary concern on Sebby's face. He had a sixth sense where supplies of food and drink were concerned.

'Excuse me, Fra,' she said, catching a signal from Sebby. 'I think the fox is among the chickens.'

The family signal for trouble made her father glance round in alarm. 'God, not the whisky!'

'We'll manage,' she soothed. Whatever happened, Rolf must not be worried—she and Sebby had a silent understanding about that.

Roddy Sumner moved away from Cleo and caught at Katrine's hand as she moved past. 'Lovely party,' he drawled. She gave him a faintly puzzled smile. He was the only member of the press who ever recognised her and she was human enough to find this very flattering, but she found it odd, too. Roddy was tall, dark and extremely good-looking, wildly popular with the opposite sex. It had occurred to Katrine that one of the less obvious reasons for his popularity was his knack of remembering everyone's name and face. It was a useful trick for a journalist, especially one who went in for light flirtations. Katrine sometimes wondered why Roddy bothered to pay her any attention, since she could not be useful to him in his career, nor was she a raving beauty.

He was looking down at her with narrowed eyes. 'You do know who I am?' he pressed quizzically.

She laughed. 'Of course! We've met dozens of times.'

'Then why do you always look at me with that

vague, puzzled little smile?' he asked.

'Do I?' She felt the colour creep up into her face. Then, with unusual bluntness, she said, 'That isn't because I don't know who *you* are. It is because I'm surprised you know who I am.'

He watched her, his expression thoughtful. 'How revealing. You're too modest, Cinderella. People take you at your own valuation, you know. If you creep off into a corner, they think you must be very dull, so they ignore you.'

Had she drunk a tiny bit more champagne than usual? she asked herself incredulously, as she heard herself answer him. 'Then why don't you?'

'Why don't I what?'

'Ignore me? You always notice me.' It must be his amused, tolerant look that was encouraging her to talk in this easy fashion, she decided.

'You interest me,' he returned blandly. 'You are so unlike the rest of your family.'

A stricken look appeared on her small face. 'I see,' she said. She gave him a frozen little smile. 'Excuse me. Sebby is making frantic signs for help.'

He frowned and caught her elbow. 'Look here, I hadn't finished explaining...'

'There's really no need,' she said brightly. 'I know perfectly well how different I am—the only ordinary one, the duckling among the swans.' She laughed. 'I'm quite used to it, you know. Don't worry about hurting my feelings.'

His glance followed her as she crossed the room, and a line creased the smoothness of Roddy Sumner's forehead. A commotion at the door then drew his attention, and he turned away as Dodie Alexander arrived, sallow and angular in wine silk yet dimming even the golden splendour of the Milfords by her sheer luminosity. Plain, quiet and lacking sex appeal, Dodie only had to walk on stage for an audience to gasp as though she had revealed some new dimension of beauty. Roddy watched her, pondering this gift—what was the secret? A quality of stillness, of sincerity? Impossible to pin it down.

She was talking, kissing Rolf, embracing the other guests with her dark, expressive eyes.

Behind her lounged a tall, supercilious man with a long, bony nose and heavy-lidded eyes, his expression amused. Dodie turned and touched his arm in a confiding gesture, intimate and warm.

Roddy gave a silent whistle, his lips pursed in surprise. Was that how the wind blew? Dodie Alexander had been happily married for ten years to Jack Sandon. His death a few months ago had been as tragic as it had been sudden. Dodie had looked like a lost soul for weeks. Was she now coming out of it, and was Max Neilson the cause of that returning radiance in her face?

Roddy made a mental note. His column was always filled with these titbits of gossip, ingenious invention or inspired guesswork. It was at parties like this that one picked up the first thread of such information.

'They're making a big hole in the whisky,' Sebby told Katrine sadly.

He had a lined, sallow face which reminded her of a clown—great, melancholy dark eyes, a large nose and a way of hunching his shoulders which spoke louder than words.

Sebby was of part Russian descent. He had been her father's dresser for years. When her mother died, soon after Katrine's tenth birthday, Sebby moved into their home to take over the running of the household. They had all been so lost, so broken that nobody had known what to do. Sebby had saved the day, and somehow he had never moved out again. That had been ten years ago. Now it seemed as if he had always been there. What would they all do without him? He was the backbone of their lives; the organiser, the home-maker.

When Katrine left school she had drifted into staying at home, helping Sebby. He had instinctively, silently known how much she dreaded getting a job, going out into the hostile world. She had had no dreams of a career. She had not even wanted to pursue her education any further. All she had wanted to do was to cook, clean, sew and keep house. She had always dreamt of being like her mother. She had such happy memories of childhood. Her mother had always been in the kitchen, making gingerbread or ironing, and Katrine sometimes had an overwhelming nostalgia for that vanished past when she smelt hot gingerbread or the clean, fresh-air smell of washing.

Her father had said in a totally audible aside to

the others, 'Thank God she doesn't want to go on the stage, poor child!'

Cleo had giggled, then smoothed out her face into its usual golden mask. 'She has always been terrifically domesticated, it's true, Fra.'

Katrine had 'understudied' Sebby for two years now, taking instruction humbly in all the domestic arts and being very careful never to offend or hurt him. She loved Sebby almost as much as she loved her father.

Now she said, 'Shall I pop out for some more?' There was an off-licence just down the road.

Someone loomed at Katrine's shoulder, handed over two bottles of whisky. 'A contribution from Dodie,' drawled a familiar voice.

Sebby's melancholy face broke into a smile. 'Thank Gawd for Madame!' He always called Dodie Madame. Katrine had never liked to ask why. She knew Sebby worshipped Dodie, but then who didn't?

'And how is little Katrine?' the voice drawled.

Reluctantly, she turned and looked up into Max Neilson's blandly mocking face. Of all the actors she had ever met, he was the most maddening. He had moved over into direction lately, and she knew that he was planning to launch a new Festival down at Cantwich, that famous home of Pascal Flint, the Edwardian playwright whose centenary was being celebrated this summer. Flint had been a drunken rascal, but two of his plays had become classics of their kind, and Cantwich was proud of the connection.

Max watched her with an amused smile. 'Congratulations on the decor,' he murmured. 'You and Sebby are quite a team.'

She looked surprised. Few people knew that she and Sebby had redecorated the room. It had taken them six weeks to strip off the fading Chinese wallpaper, re-paint the woodwork and the ceiling and then give the walls a smooth coating of eau-de-nil paint. The result was charming. They had transformed the room into a replica of an eighteenth-century Adam room—classical, restrained and elegant. The carpet and curtains had been changed, and Rolf had moaned at the expense of it all, but he, too, was happy with the result. He was particularly happy with the marble fireplace. Today a great spray of summer flowers filled it, but in winter it became the glowing centre of the room, the flickering firelight transforming it.

'How is your festival coming along?' she asked politely.

'Dodie is playing Ianthe in *Hazard Green*,' he told her.

'I'm sure that will be a great success,' she nodded. The play was always popular, and Dodie was a great favourite with the public.

'And I want Rolf and Cleo to come down and do *Button Man* for me,' he added.

She looked taken aback. 'Good heavens! Rolf is a little old for the lead and...'

'I want him to do the button man,' Max told her, watching her face.

She looked horrified. 'Have you told him?'

'Not yet. You think he'll refuse?'

'It is rather a small part.'

'It is the title role,' he pointed out.

'He only appears in the last act, though,' she said.

'It's of symbolic significance, though,' Max said lightly.

She grimaced. 'Rather you than me.'

'You think he'll be annoyed?'

'Insulted,' she said bluntly.

Max laughed. 'I do believe you're right. We'll see.' He changed the subject. 'Your friend Nicky will be at Cantwich with us, playing the boy in *Hazard Green*.'

She flushed. 'How nice. Why do you say "my friend"? He's a friend of the whole family.'

'Particularly yours, I think,' drawled Max. 'And I got the impression not at all a friend of Cleo's—indeed, I fancy she detests him.'

'Oh, Cleo,' she dismissed. 'She was cross because...' Then she caught herself up, flushing.

'Because?' he probed, curious.

Because Nicky did not fall madly in love with her on sight, she had been about to say before she realised to whom she had been about to say it. Family loyalty dictated silence. She gave him a polite little shake of the head. 'Nothing. Dodie is looking for you, I think...' Glancing over his shoulder.

Dodie joined them, her dark eyes smiling warmly

at Katrine, whom she had known since Katrine was a tiny girl of six. 'Darling Katya ...' She had always called her that. Dodie was, like Sebby, part Russian, and she had a habit of turning names into Russian, half from a love of the sound of them, half to make them sound different, individual, exciting. 'How are you? You look very sweet and good in that little dress, but you ought to get Cleo to help you choose something more sophisticated for these occasions. You let those sisters of yours outshine you.' She shook a gentle finger at her. 'You must not let them upstage you, darling Katya. You can be as dazzling as any of them. Any woman can if she tries! Beauty is only artificial, after all. It is in the eye of the beholder—and it can be put on or taken off like a coat!'

Katrine smiled at her. 'Yes, dear Dodie!'

Dodie was not deceived. She shook her head ruefully. 'Ah, you are placating me. You will stay as you are! Mulish child!'

'She is very well as she is,' Max drawled. 'There are enough Milfords shining in the firmament as it is. Leave the child alone, Dodie.'

Dodie eyed him. 'What do you know, Max? Men know nothing of these things, they do not understand the heart of a woman.'

Katrine discreetly slipped away to join Sebby once more. He was pouring pink gins for a crowd of thirsty reporters. They looked at Katrine with piercing indifference, took their glasses and vanished, en masse, for the other side of the room and

Cleo. Golden, amused and lively, she was putting on a wonderful performance for them, making them roar with laughter and eye her amorously all at once.

'I've been pushing the gin,' Sebby told her. 'I think we may hold out. Madame saved us with her two bottles. Time some of this lot were moving on, anyway.'

'I'm tired,' Katrine told him. 'Someone has made a burn mark on the grand piano and there's ash on the carpet beside the fireplace.' She sighed.

'And Max Neilson has arrived,' Sebby nodded wryly. 'I saw him buttonhole you. Can't stand him, can you?'

'He's so bored and omniscient—a bit like God, only too worldly.'

'He's clever,' Sebby observed.

'Oh, that, yes—too clever, if you ask me. He frightens me rather.'

'I hear he's been very good to Madame since her husband died,' Sebby murmured. Anyone who was kind to Dodie would be forgiven much by Sebby. To him Dodie Alexander was little short of divinity.

'Perhaps he's in love with her,' said Katrine, giggling. The thought of Max in love seemed very funny, wildly improbable.

Sebby gave her an affronted glare, but just then some new guests drifted up to get their glasses filled and Katrine seized the chance to escape.

So Nicky was going to be in Cantwich all summer

long, she thought ruefully. He hadn't told her. How long had he known? It was entirely typical that he should keep it a secret until it was unavoidable to tell her—Nicky knew it would upset her.

A flush crept over her throat and cheeks at the thought. Nicky knew only too well how she felt about him. Why must I be so obvious? she asked herself despairingly. I should have hidden it better, been less of a pushover.

Perhaps it was because Nicky had all the golden good looks of a true Milford—he was a second cousin, in fact. She had known him all her life, but had only fallen head over heels in love last year. They had all been on holiday in Provence. The long hot days, the sandy beaches, the starry nights had set the scene for romance in the old-fashioned traditional sense—and Katrine, nineteen years old and eager for life, had looked at Nicky with new-found eyes and fallen in love with him.

At first she had believed her love returned. Nicky had held her hand, walked with her in the warm, breathing darkness of the villa garden and kissed her with gentle tenderness. Cleo's sharp, mocking eyes had soon found out their secret, and her witty tongue had teased them unmercifully. Cleo, although she did not want Nicky for herself, was affronted because he had never even shown a passing interest in her. Accustomed to her power over the men who visited them, Cleo found it galling that Nicky should prefer her shy, ordinary little sister to herself.

Since their return to London, Katrine had noticed a change in Nicky. He always kissed her when they met, and she saw quite a lot of him, but his whole attitude was casual, affectionate rather than loving, and he showed no desire to move into a deeper, more personal relationship. Herself fathoms deep in love, Katrine felt the difference acutely. She tried to hide from him her own passionate response, but she sensed that Nicky was quite aware of how she felt towards him.

She caught a glimpse of herself in one of the gilded mirrors lining the wall, at regular intervals, and saw a thin, pale girl with a red spot burning on each cheek and great, dark-lashed blue eyes fixed in unhappy reverie. Self-hatred filled her. She looked at her reflection with loathing. Why had she not been born one of the 'Magnificent Milfords'? Why had she alone, out of the family, been born with dull brown hair and such ordinary features?

She turned away, biting her lip. Nicky would have loved her had she been beautiful, she thought.

Dodie Alexander, catching the agony in the movement, said suddenly to Max Neilson, 'That child is unhappy. Where did she find that appalling dress? It makes her look like a gauche schoolgirl. She has good bone structure and fine eyes. With a little help she could look quite striking. I've tried to push her in the right direction several times, but the obstinate little creature refuses to budge.'

'She refuses to compete,' he drawled. 'If you were the youngest Milford you'd sympathise, I imagine.

You would either have to fight like a demon to come out on top—or withdraw altogether.'

'Which is what Katya has done?' Dodie's dark eyes looked up at him intelligently. 'Yes, I think you are right, darling.'

'I always am,' he returned with casual arrogance.

'Yes, that is what is so maddening about you,' she agreed. 'The child detests you, doesn't she?'

He looked down his long nose and smiled sleepily. 'All her emotions are written on her face, aren't they? Such an expressive little face.'

Dodie looked suddenly struck. 'Yes,' she said, on a long-drawn-out note. 'With features like those she should have been an actress. Odd that she opted out.'

'I have told you the reason,' he pointed out.

'So you did, darling. What a tragic waste, though. Something should be done about it.'

'No doubt something will,' he drawled enigmatically.

Roddy Sumner slid through the crowd and joined them, smiling ingratiatingly. 'You're looking enchanting tonight, Dodie,' he said, kissing her hand with natural grace.

She looked at Max over Roddy's bent head. The dark eyes laughed. 'Thank you. darling,' she drawled. 'Has Max told you his plans for his Festival? You must hear about it ...'

Cass Milford moved over to Katrine. 'You're looking a bit fraught, angel. Anything wrong? Don't say the whisky is running dry? Shall I nip out and get some?'

She turned on a smile. 'No, Sebby has things under control, but thanks for offering. Viola's enjoying herself, isn't she?'

They looked across the room. Viola was dancing energetically with a slim young man in a green shirt. He was laughing, but Katrine saw something very serious behind the smile in his blue eyes.

'I'm afraid poor old Geoff Farmer is badly smitten,' Cass said easily. 'Just as well his dad is on the way to his first million—any man who marries Viola will need pots of money.'

'You think she'll marry Geoff?' Katrine was not quite so certain. Viola was basically such a frivolous person. Katrine could not ever remember being in love. Viola had clowned, drawled, teased her way through life. She was witty, charming, energetic and totally selfish.

While they watched, though, Geoffrey Farmer stopped dancing and looked down at Viola with an expression which even the most purblind mole would have recognised as besotted. He took her hands and held them, then gave a strangled whoop and swung round, almost knocking over Rolf Milford.

Beaming, babbling, Geoffrey spoke to his host, and Rolf stared from him to Viola and back again, then he took Viola's face and held it between his two hands, kissing her with paternal reverence upon the brow in a gesture which was theatrically moving and yet quite sincere at the same time.

'Everybody!' he shouted, holding up a hand for silence. 'Listen, everybody—the most wonderful, delightful news! My dearest child, Viola, is to be married...'

Someone groaned, and everybody laughed. The piano player broke spontaneously into 'Here Comes the Bride...' Cleo flung herself upon Viola, arms spread wide, crying, 'Darling, how heavenly!'

Then everyone crowded round the happy couple and the noise in the room redoubled. Katrine looked up at Cass, grimacing. 'You were absolutely right, after all. Imagine! Viola in love!'

'What makes you say she's in love? I said Geoff was in love. I didn't say anything about Viola.'

'But, Cass, she accepted him,' protested Katrine.

'So?'

'She must be in love with him,' said Katrine. 'Why else should she marry him?'

'I can think of many reasons,' Cass drawled. 'Almost a million of them, in fact.'

'Cynicism, my dear fellow, cynicism,' drawled an amused voice behind them.

Katrine felt herself go pink with indignation and hostility. It was that horrid, sarcastic Max Neilson again, she thought, giving him a sparkling glance. 'Well, I don't believe anyone would marry just for money,' she told them both crossly. 'Viola earns quite a lot, you know. She doesn't need to marry money.'

'Viola spends quite a lot, too,' Cass said lightly.

'Why, she's more extravagant than Cleo, and that's saying something!'

'Your little sister has illusions about romance,' drawled Max. 'Don't shatter them, Cass. The young cherish their illusions.'

'I was young last year,' Cass said with a sigh. 'It was hell.' He gave them a shared smile and slipped away.

'I see your brother is cultivating the world-weary pose at present,' Max said in amusement.

'Cass has always been difficult to understand,' Katrine said with a little twist of her shoulder, as though she would have loved to turn her back on him yet in courtesy could not do so.

'He's very intelligent,' Max observed.

'Oh, don't be so patronising!' Katrine snapped, then went bright pink.

Max laughed.

Katrine gave him a silent, angry look, then said in a cold voice, 'Excuse me, I must go and congratulate Viola.'

'She deserves to be congratulated,' he agreed coolly. 'She's played her fish expertly. Very pretty angling indeed. I've enjoyed watching. I only hope she finds the result as satisfying as she thinks she will.'

'I think you're a perfect beast!' Katrine burst out, and rushed away from him with a furious expression.

Katrine and Sebby cleared up after the party, working together in amicable silence until the room had been returned to something like normal.

Katrine was very tired when she fell into bed, but she could not sleep. Her mind kept presenting her with images. She saw Viola's face as she looked at her new fiancé. She saw Max smiling in sardonic amusement. She saw Cass, looking remote and cynical. The tangle of impressions made no sense, yet somehow she felt that there was a common thread in them somehow, if only she knew how to find the end of it, pull it and unravel it.

CHAPTER TWO

THE morning after one of their parties the house was always like a morgue. Katrine and Sebby silently pursued their normal routine while the others slept. Polishing the furniture in the long drawing-room, Katrine felt her usual pleasure as she watched the pale flecks of dust float upward in a golden stream of light from the window. The dreamy, summer sense of quietness persisted particularly at the back of the house. Tall, narrow and elegant, the house had been built in 1819 by a merchant banker. His totally invented coat of arms ornamented the stucco over the portico, and his view of the position of the servant class was demonstrated by the vast gulf between the size of the reception rooms on the first floor and the attic bedrooms which had been intended for the servants.

The long, flat windows of the drawing-room looked out over the green garden, past rose beds and lawns, to the river showing deceptively green through the branches of a willow. At close hand the water was muddy, foully odorous and filled with debris, but if one did not look too close it made an enchanting backcloth on a sunny summer morning, with the sunlight dancing on the surface and the occasional sight of a boat to enliven the view.

Viola had asked to be called at ten o'clock. Katrine took her up a tray: orange juice, a slice of French toast and black coffee. Viola sat up, yawning. 'Is it ten already? God...'

'Shall I start your shower?' Katrine offered.

'Not yet.' Viola sat up, hugging her thin knees, a primrose cotton sheet wrapped round her. Her hair fell immaculately into place, the cut so exquisite that it barely needed combing. 'What do you think of Geoff?' She watched her sister intently.

'He seems very nice.' Katrine did not know what to say. She hardly knew him. She remembered what Cass had said. Was Viola marrying him for his money? Or had Cass been merely malicious, teasing for fun?

Oddly, Viola seemed to seize upon the word with eagerness. 'Nice. Yes, isn't he? I'm glad you like him.' She looked at her sister through her own pale lashes, her false ones lying neatly in their box upon the dressing-table. The sun, streaming through the raised window, turned the ends of her lashes to bright gold. 'Be friendly to him, darling, will you? I feel a bit like Daniel's mother watching him walk into the lions' den—I remember you always called us the Milford lions. Do you remember that? You were such a funny, solemn little girl.'

Katrine felt her spirits lift. Viola's concern for Geoff could, surely, only mean a fondness for him. It was understandable that she should be worried. Cass and Cleo were not ones to suffer fools gladly, and Katrine suspected they would write Geoffrey Farmer down an ass. Indeed, Viola herself had before now been known to show a lazy scorn towards people like Geoffrey. Her own quick wits, dry humour and clever mockery made her a natural scourge towards anyone who could not keep up with her. Katrine had come in for some pretty merciless teasing in the past. She knew how Viola's tongue could sting.

Rolf had his breakfast next, always the same, a pot of tea and two rolls with butter and black cherry jam—a peculiar mixture of England and continental breakfast. 'I must give a dinner party for Viola and her husband-to-be,' he said. 'Just family, do you think, Katrine? Or a few friends, too?'

'You must ask Dodie,' she pointed out.

'And she'll want to bring Max Neilson, I suppose,' Rolf agreed, a little tartly. 'What does she see in him, my dear? He's younger than Dodie and so terribly, depressingly clever.' He pushed away his tray. 'So, I am at leisure from this morning. A delightful opportunity to relax and enjoy my life. I shall dress and go for a stroll. Shopping—that is what I shall do, shopping. I need some new ties, new socks. My shirts are in rags.'

She glanced wryly at his open wardrobe, fitted along one side of his bedroom, jammed with clothes. 'Poor Fra! Quite reduced to tatters.'

'Don't you turn sarcastic on me, my girl,' he said with dignity. 'How else am I to occupy myself?' A note of deep sadness entered his voice. It swelled to an organ note. 'Othello's occupation's gone ...'

'Oh, dear,' she said, whisking his tray away. She knew that look.

Sebby was chopping boiled eggs. He intended to make a cold mousse for lunch. In summer they sometimes ate on the patio under the green shade of a pear tree.

'He's restless already,' she told Sebby as she began to wash up. Cleo and Cass had been taken their trays —both of them took the lightest breakfast, orange juice and black coffee. They would have shuddered if they had ever risen early enough to see Katrine and Sebby tucking into their hearty breakfast of egg and bacon, and toast and marmalade, at seven-thirty, washed down by cup after cup of tea from a vast powder blue pot which Sebby kept drinkable by constant additions of hot water. But then, as Sebby said, after Katrine had once made some remark upon it, they needed a good meal on which to face a day of constant domestic toil.

Sebby glanced up, his great dark eyes sharp. 'Why not ring Mr Neilson? He could have lunch here.'

'The Festival? Oh, can you see Fra's face when

Max tells him he wants him to play the button man? He'll roar like the big bad wolf.'

'Give him something to roar about, though,' Sebby said. 'Nothing makes him so cross as being out of work.'

'He only started being out of work this morning,' she pointed out. 'He isn't desperate yet.'

'Give him twenty minutes and he will be,' Sebby nodded.

It was true. Rolf felt like a lost soul when he was not working. She hesitated, then went to the phone.

Max answered himself, but she pretended not to recognise his voice. It would have flattered him too much. 'Could I speak to Mr Neilson?'

'You are doing, my girl,' he returned maddeningly, at once seeing through her pretence and acknowledging her.

She stubbornly persisted. 'This is Katrine Milford, Mr Neilson.'

'I'm aware of that,' he drawled. 'What time shall I come over?'

His omniscience disgusted her. 'We lunch at one o'clock,' she said flatly. 'Say ... twelve-thirty?'

He laughed. 'Try not to be so cross when I arrive. Can I help it if I have second sight?'

'How *did* you know why I'd rung?'

'I know Rolf. He hates unemployment. You haven't mentioned my idea to him yet?'

'No,' she conceded. 'I thought it would be best if you brought that up.'

'Oh, wise young judge,' he mocked. 'Cowardly, too. What are we having for lunch?'

'Salmon mayonnaise, a savoury mousse and summer pudding,' she told him.

'Summer pudding? Delicious! I haven't eaten that for years. What fruit are you using for it?'

'Raspberries and red currants,' she said.

'I can't wait,' he said, ringing off.

She replaced the receiver very carefully. Sebby looked at her when she returned to the kitchen, noting her red cheeks. 'You look very hot. Why don't you go out into the garden for half an hour and cool off in the shade?'

'And feed the midges? No, thanks,' she said. 'I'll get the fruit ready for the pudding.' Sebby had already done the shopping at his favourite shops. It was one of his most enjoyable occupations, strolling leisurely along with a basket on his arm, tucking asparagus or smoked salmon, eggs or lamb chops, new potatoes or strawberries in together, gossiping with the shopkeepers whom he knew intimately, meeting old friends from the neighbourhood and inspecting any new arrivals with a cold, beady eye. Winter or summer, Sebby liked to do what he called 'my marketing' at the same hour of the day.

When she had prepared the fruit Sebby shooed her out of the back door, a cup of coffee in one hand, a magazine in the other, to take a brief break in the garden. Rolf had already gone out, having been warned of Max's imminent arrival and promising to be back well in time. Cleo came out in a brief sundress and a bottle of sun-tan oil.

'I must just have half an hour out here. I don't want my tan to fade,' she said, stretching out on a multi-coloured towel.

'Max is coming to lunch,' Katrine told her.

'Is he?' Cleo opened one eye. 'How heavenly. I hope he isn't bringing Dodie.'

'How can you be so horrid? Dodie's an angel.'

'So everyone says. I've yet to see her wings.' Cleo smoothed oil into one sleek golden leg. 'Imagine Viola marrying that big bore! Can you believe it? I shudder at the idea.'

'I think she's very fond of him,' Katrina said cautiously.

Cleo was bent in graceful self-absorption, like a cat at its toilette, worshipping the beauty of her own body. Her fingers stroked and smoothed gently along her skin.

'You're so naïve,' she said absently. 'Viola's far too selfish to care for anyone. I'd have thought even you must know that.'

Hadn't that been what Katrine really thought until this morning? Yet now she could not help remembering something about Viola's face that made her spring now to her sister's defence. 'All the same, I think she does care for him.'

'Cares for his money, you mean,' said Cleo.

Stung, Katrine said on a sudden impulse, 'If you aren't careful your freckles will come back, in this bright sunlight.'

Cleo looked up, astonished. 'Miaow! So the kitten has claws? Who'd have thought it?' Then she laughed, all her cynical, lazy sophistication falling away. 'Do you remember those summers when we were at school? My little dinghy? I don't think I've ever been as happy since. Those hours we spent fishing and sailing up and down! Absolute heaven.'

They relaxed in happy silence for a while, until Katrine had to go in to help Sebby with the vegetables. They worked fast, making a dressing for the salad, chopping parsley and slicing tomatoes. Rolf came back with Max, whom he had picked up a few yards from their door, and they settled down on the tiny patio to eat the cold meal on a white-painted iron table. Max had brought some very good white wine. The pear tree made a gently shifting shade around them. A thrush sleepily whirred overhead. Cass was out to lunch. Viola had unexpectedly brought Geoffrey along at the last moment, and he made an uneasy sixth around the table.

'Gorgeous food,' he said, raising his wine glass in a toast to Katrine.

'I'm glad you like it,' she said, smiling at him, trying to make him feel more at home and, without knowing, suddenly displaying her own version of the Milford charm in her great, dark-lashed eyes.

Geoffrey looked quite surprised, his mouth widening to a circle. He had never really noticed the little sister before, but now he decided that she was really quite endearing. She wasn't beautiful, but she had something ...

Max, glancing up, gave her an acute look. 'Not flirting with your future brother-in-law, I hope?'

She shot him a furious look, turned up her nose and did not deign to reply.

He laughed, much amused by this. Viola put her small hand over Geoffrey's much larger one, measuring them with an odd expression, and said lightly, 'Darling Max, don't tease my little sister too much.'

Cleo laughed in sudden memory of that morning's altercation. 'No, Max, let sleeping dogs lie. You won't believe this, but Katrine can bite quite sharply when she's roused.'

'Oh, I believe it,' he drawled, watching Katrine. 'But I'm astonished you've discovered it. I thought you all under-estimated her.'

Geoffrey was looking increasingly nervous at this odd form of bickering. Katrine helped him quietly to another portion of the mousse, spooned some Tomate Niçoise on to his plate and poured him some more wine.

He gave her a grateful look. Despite his healthy skin, broad shoulders and generally vigorous air, Katrine decided, there was something of the little boy about him. She wondered, suddenly, if it could be this that had drawn Viola to him, but a doubt alarmed her. She looked secretly at her sister, tracing the wicked curl of her pretty mouth, the strong line of jaw and nose, the slanting green eyes. There was absolutely nothing maternal about Viola. Why was she marrying Geoffrey Farmer?

Max broached the subject of his Festival, and

mentioned the idea of doing *Button Man*. Cleo looked interested at once. There was a very exciting role in it for her, and she gave Max a flutter of her lashes, a come-hither look from her bright eyes.

'No need to try seduction, my sweet,' he drawled. 'I want to audition you. I thought of you for Anna at once.'

'Formal audition?' she asked.

'There is a Festival committee,' he explained, half apologetically. 'I have the final vote, but purely as a formality I have to parade my casts for them.'

'Aren't you the director?' she asked, raising an ironic eyebrow and smiling very sweetly at him.

'You know how these things work,' he said. 'One must placate the locals.'

'Hand out a few strings of beads if the natives get restless,' Viola murmured.

Rolf was bored. He pushed his plate away. Katrine got up and went in to get the summer pudding. The whipped cream and the pink shading of the pudding itself looked delicious as she carried them out. Sebby was sitting at the kitchen table eating the left-over mousse, some spoonfuls of caviar which he had used to decorate it, and some vegetables. 'Save a slice for me,' he asked.

'Of course I will,' she said, indignantly. 'When do we ever eat it all?'

'That Geoffrey Farmer looks like a pig to me,' Sebby said darkly.

'He likes his food,' she admitted. 'But he's very nice.'

Sebby grunted.

'The mousse was as light and cool as a cloud,' she flattered.

He looked at her out of his great, melancholy dark eyes. 'Of course it was,' he said scornfully, pushing away her pitiful attempt at placation.

When she got back Rolf was pacing up and down, purple in the face, exploding at intervals, 'Play what? Play what? I'm a walk-on now, am I? I know I'm getting old, but this is insulting...'

'It's the title role,' said Max, grinning at Katrine as she thumped the pudding down in the centre of the table and gave him a look of 'I told you so...'

She began to serve the soft, melting pudding, the fruit falling out on to the plates as she did so. Geoffrey looked at it with a rapt expression. 'Did you make this?' He sounded incredulous.

'Before we go any further I'd better tell you I can't cook,' said Viola carelessly. 'And I'm not going to learn. I hate cooking and I hate food.'

Geoffrey laughed. 'We can always eat out,' he said cheerfully, tucking into the pudding.

'You've got some cream on your nose,' Viola said, leaning over to dab at him with her napkin.

For a second their faces were close together, their eyes gazing into each other, and Katrine, seized by immobility, saw with a fast-beating heart a look pass between them which both relieved and excited her. Even her sheltered innocence could recognise the look of passion.

Katrine took the pudding back into the house,

aware that Geoffrey pursued it with an agonised look. Sebby spooned it on to his clean plate.

'You nearly didn't get any,' Katrine said, laughing.

'That Geoffrey,' muttered Sebby.

'Yes, I thought he was going to snatch it away from me. Poor him, though, married to Viola. She eats two lettuce leaves and a glass of orange juice and feels full up. He'll starve.'

'He can always learn to cook,' Sebby said indifferently.

'With all his money? That isn't likely.' She began to carry out the coffee. 'Perhaps they'll have a cook.'

Geoffrey met her at the kitchen door, almost making her drop the tray. 'I say, is there any of that pudding left?' He peered past her and saw Sebby hurriedly eating the last mouthfuls. 'Oh ...' His face fell. 'Is that your marvellous cook? I must congratulate him!'

While he flattered Sebby, she carried the coffee out. Max took it from her, grinning down at her. 'I suspect Farmer has gone in to poach Sebby from you.'

She was unalarmed. 'He's optimistic. It would take an atom bomb to dislodge Sebby.'

Viola gave a little smile. 'Geoffrey has more to him than you think! He can be very persuasive.'

Cleo and Rolf hooted. 'It's beyond human capacity to tempt Sebby from this house,' Rolf boasted.

'Will you lay me ten to one?' Viola taunted.

Rolf produced a pound note and put it on the

table, smoothing it out. 'Done.'

Max laughed. 'This is a new side to you, Viola! Your faith in your future husband is touching.'

She was unabashed. 'You'll learn to appreciate him.'

'Well, you did,' conceded Cleo, yawning. Her eyes threw her sister an unspoken message: I can't imagine why! And Viola gave her a little grimace in return, a shrug of her slender shoulders.

Geoffrey trailed back to them, his air of despondency bringing a smile to Cleo's face. She looked at her sister, raising a thin eyebrow.

'Ten to one, you said,' Rolf murmured, rubbing thumb and finger together in an inviting manner.

Viola looked at Geoffrey. He shook his head.

'I offered him three times what your father gives him, but he turned me down flat.'

Rolf crowed. 'What did I tell you? Even Dodie Alexander has never prised Sebby loose from me, so I knew you wouldn't manage it, my boy.' He beamed upon him. 'Not that I hold it against you for trying! No, no.' He looked at Viola. 'Pay up, my girl.'

She paid, reluctantly, and then she and Geoffrey left to meet some friends. Katrine poured the coffee. The remainder of the party sat about, sleepily relaxed, listening to the slap slap of the river, the whisper of the trees overhead, the far-off roar of London traffic which sounded oddly like the sea.

Max coolly reintroduced the subject of *Button Man*, and Rolf glared at him. Katrine got up from her chair and stretched out upon the grass under a tree. Sleep hung upon her lids and a drowsy sweetness crept over her body. She felt oddly happy. The sounds, scents and colours of the summer garden seemed to mingle and become one feeling, a sensation of joy which ran through her veins and invaded every limb.

Something tickled her nose. She irritably brushed it away, but it returned, and she opened her eyes to find Max leaning beside her, a piece of grass in his hand. He had been tickling her with it.

'Where is everyone?' she asked in surprise, looking past him at the empty patio.

'Rolf has gone off to some appointment. Cleo had to see a man about some shoes. You've been asleep.' The heavy-lidded eyes surveyed her mockingly. 'You look about ten years old when you're asleep. Did you know?'

Flushed and conscious of dishevelment, she sat up. 'I must go and help Sebby. There's such a lot to do.'

'Your father has agreed to take the role,' he drawled.

She stared. 'No! You aren't serious?'

'Wait and see. It will be a critical success. A perfect cameo performance.'

She stared at the peaceful profile of the house, the flat windows, ancient brickwork and stucco slumbering in the afternoon sunlight. 'So you'll have both Cleo and Fra.'

'And Nicky,' he murmured. 'Surely you haven't

forgotten the adorable Nicky?'

Her cheeks burned. She avoided his watchful stare. He saw altogether too much. 'Quite a Milford Festival,' she said lightly.

'You must come down for the summer, too,' he said. 'The run will last six weeks. You must take a house. Bring Sebby.'

'We'll never find one at such short notice,' she said. 'By now they'll all be taken.'

'Then you must all share mine,' he said. 'I've taken a house there. There are five bedrooms, plenty of room.'

'Why did you take one of that size?' she asked in surprise.

'I thought it might come in useful,' he returned evasively. 'One always has visitors at these things.'

Katrine's heart was beating so fast she wondered if he heard it. She would be spending six weeks close to Nicky. They might even reproduce the glorious intimacy of last summer, the romantic evenings in the countryside, the candlelit suppers and lazy walks by moonlight.

Max was watching her, his long nose wrinkled in disgust. 'What a blatant little romantic you are! How did you come to be born into this armour-plated family of yours? You're about as thick-skinned as a soft-boiled egg.'

'Eggs have shells,' she reminded him.

'But you don't,' he said drily. 'One day you're going to get badly hurt if you exhibit your feelings to all and sundry in this foolish fashion!'

'Will Dodie be at Cantwich?' she asked, ignoring his previous remarks.

'Yes, and sharing my house, too, so you can act as chaperone, my child.' He gave her a cool smile, his expression gently mocking.

'Don't call me that!' she flared.

'What? My child? It is something of an impossibility, I suppose,' he drawled. 'There can only be a matter of fifteen years between us, and although I was of course highly precocious it didn't happen to be in that particular direction. I was referring less to your age, however, as to your mental development. You're curiously retarded in some ways.'

'Thanks very much,' she said bitterly.

He laughed. 'I fancy this is going to be a highly instructive summer. What an oddly assorted collection we shall be!'

Rolf was a great deal more cheerful next morning. He sang in his shower so loudly that their neighbours banged on the wall. Since their neighbour was a famous conductor Rolf took this as a compliment and sang louder, driving that eminent gentleman to a positive frenzy in which he rang the house to scream insults down the telephone.

'I am so sorry, Signor Tossetti,' Katrine murmured soothingly. 'I'm afraid my father is unhappy today.'

She thought he would take this better than a confession that Rolf was ecstatic with renewal, brimming with new zest.

'Unhappy?' Signor Tossetti screeched. 'I thought he was dying!'

Over lunch Rolf delivered a beautiful impression of Tossetti to a hysterical audience. They wept with laughter and Rolf beamed. He had brought back four old friends to lunch without warning Sebby, who was sulkily clashing pans in the kitchen.

Katrine soothed him. 'You know what Fra is like.'

'Thoughtless,' Sebby snapped. 'If I'd known Jack Beale was coming I could have made Veal Napoli—it's his favourite. But I hadn't a slice of veal in the house. Just ham and cheese. What can you do with that?'

'You did a beautiful soufflé,' Katrine flattered. 'The best I've ever seen, and they scraped the dish clean.'

'Just as well I made two, then,' he returned, unmoved, and took it from the oven all golden and light as an angel's kiss.

'Fra is so happy to be working again. What is it about him that he can't be happy even for one day if he isn't working?'

'Some are like that,' Sebby said with a shrug. 'Your father needs the theatre. Without it he feels empty.' He glanced at her. 'Young Nicky's the same —a chip off the old block. Far more than Cass is— Nicky and your father have a lot in common.'

'Do you think so?' She was taken aback. It had never occurred to her.

'Think about it,' Sebby said, almost gently.

'Hello, gang,' said Viola, appearing at the door, radiant in white jersey silk which gave a new seduction to her slight body. She had never possessed Cleo's glowing sensuality, but to Katrine's eye she seemed now to be transfigured with happiness into something approaching real beauty.

She swept Katrine up to her bedroom to look at some clothes she had just bought.

'Do you think long engagements are a good thing?' she asked. displaying a pair of clinging green pants with which she planned to wear a tight matching top.

'Depends on the people concerned,' Katrina returned.

Viola sank on her bed and stared at herself in the mirror. 'I don't see the point of waiting. Geoff and I are quite certain. Why bother to have the full palaver of a big wedding? Why not just a register office and dash for it?'

Katrine sat down beside her and looked at her thoughtfully. 'You could do that, of course, but personally I would feel cheated. Your wedding day is, we hope, a once-in-a-lifetime day. It ought to be something utterly fantastic. A day to remember. Like fireworks or a circus, or the first time you see a rainbow.'

'Yes,' Viola said slowly. 'Perhaps you're right. But it will take weeks to arrange everything. All that work, all those plans. Decisions, decisions ... What hymns to have. What flowers. What bridesmaids. It's endless.'

'But it only happens once in your whole life,' said Katrine. 'Think of first nights! The excitement, the hard work.'

'The pain in your stomach,' added Viola wryly. 'I'm always sick on first nights. I get migraine for twelve hours beforehand, then I'm sick just before curtain up.'

Katrine was amazed. 'I never knew that!' She stared at her sister.

'Why should you? I didn't broadcast the fact. I found it utterly shaming, to tell you the truth.'

Katrine looked at her; the shrewd, slanting eyes, the clever bright mouth, the feathery curls. Behind the vivid surface another Viola had existed all this time, and Katrine had never even known it. Now, suddenly, she was beginning to find out these things about her, as if Viola had suddenly let down the veil between them, exposing her true self to her sister.

Just as Viola was about to marry and go away, Katrine began to feel she could grow very fond of her. What a waste, she thought. Of course, Viola was much older than her. They had always been separated by those years. Viola had always been several steps ahead.

Is she still far ahead, or am I catching up at last? She looked at her sister with wistful eyes. 'You don't need to worry about the work,' she told her. 'Sebby and I will see to it.'

Viola laughed. 'Has anyone ever told you you're an angel? We'll all pull together, I promise. I shan't shirk. If Geoff and I must go through the ritual then we'll do it properly.' She stood to sardonic attention, half serious, half joking. 'Ours not to reason why, ours but to do and die ...'

'Or die,' corrected Katrine.

Viola laughed. 'There speaks a true Milford! I fluffed it! How utterly shameful! Fra would cast me off if he knew!'

Katrine got out her diary. 'Let's see about dates. It certainly can't come off until autumn because of this wretched Festival. We must consult the Vicar. Where did you think of having it? I suppose St George's. We were all christened there.'

'I'll ring and see if I can fix a date with him,' Viola promised. 'We don't need to worry about Geoff, thank God. He never does anything much at weekends, just plays golf and goes to parties. My revue closes in five weeks and I shall be free.'

They narrowed it down to a string of possible dates, and then left it, since they could get no further without consulting the Vicar of St George's, their parish church.

'I do hope I shan't be sick on this first night,' Viola said, half laughing, half desperate. 'Poor Geoff otherwise!'

'Geoff looks to me like a man who's just won the football pools,' Katrine said frankly. 'He couldn't look happier if he tried.'

Viola laughed. 'He is rather obvious, poor darling.' She gave Katrine a grin. 'I'm fairly contented myself.'

'I had noticed,' Katrine nodded.

They both laughed. Viola gave Katrine a quick pat on the hand. 'You know, we could be very good friends,' she said, half shyly.

'Yes,' said Katrine simply, smiling back. 'And I'm glad.'

CHAPTER THREE

THE Cantwich Festival was to begin in August. It was now late May and the publicity machine had long been at work, grinding out posters and leaflets, but the stars who were to appear in the two plays had not been announced, although some names had been whispered around the theatre world. When the news broke that Rolf Milford was to play the small, if symbolically important, role of the Button Man, there was considerable interest. Rolf Milford was one of the old school of theatrical stars, and for him to take such a minor role was something of a departure.

'Of course he has been branching out lately,' Viola reminded her sisters one evening. 'He took that black comedy part. That surprised me. But he was still the big cheese in that. How did Max manage to talk him into it?'

'Oh, quite a charmer when he likes, our Max,' Cleo murmured, lounging against the cushions on the chaise-longue.

Katrine collected their coffee cups and set off for

the kitchen. She was not eager to listen to a discussion of Max Neilson's charm. She doubted if he had any.

Sebby was washing up, staring at nothing. 'If the rest of us are to be down at Cantwich, what about Cass and Viola?'

'They'll stay here,' she said easily, picking up a tea towel and beginning to wipe up. 'It'll be a chance for her to practise being a housewife.'

'What, Viola? She's never done a hand's turn around here,' said Sebby with scorn. 'God knows what the place would look like when we got back.'

'Give her a chance,' Katrine said gently.

When approached, Viola was oddly taken aback. 'I suppose I could do it,' she said doubtfully. 'I suppose I'll have to run the house when I'm married.' She laughed, flushing. 'I'll do my best, anyway. Katrine, could you give a few tips? I'd hate to ask Sebby. He's so scornful.'

They spent the next Sunday together. Katrine drew up a list of jobs which ought to be done daily or weekly; how to parcel up the laundry, how to clean the windows and so on. Viola listened with a comical, despairing expression.

'What a lot of things there are to do,' she moaned. 'How do you ever get it all done?'

'It gets done somehow,' assured Katrine. 'So long as you keep the glass and china dusted, the windows clean and the carpets vacuumed, things should look quite good. These other jobs are important, too.' She read out the list. 'Really, it's just a question of drudgery rather than skill. It will give you an insight into how the house is run, though, and when you're married you will know what you're doing instead of being at a loss.'

Viola gave her a grimace. 'Do you want to bet on that? You and Sebby obviously work like slaves. I had no idea there was so much to running a house.'

A few days later they packed a dozen suitcases into the very capacious boot of Rolf's Roll's-Royce and set off for Cantwich. Cleo was cross and sleepy. The early morning was never her best time of day, and she had rather foolishly gone to a party the night before, so her eyes were red with lack of sleep and her mouth turned down at the edges.

Katrine had gone into Viola's bedroom to give her the keys. Viola had been lying, wakeful, against her lilac sheets, her blonde curls as always incredibly unruffled by the night.

'I'm nervous,' she told Katrine. 'I feel the way I do before a first night. There are butterflies in my tummy.'

'You'll sail through it,' Katrine promised her.

Viola had invited Geoffrey to dinner for that evening, and Katrine had shown her how to make omelettes. They were to have hors d'oeuvres to start with and a caramel creme to follow. It was a simple meal, but Viola was certain some disaster would overtake her.

Reassuring her, Katrine suddenly heard Rolf bellowing crossly in the hall, 'Are you coming, girl?'

She had given Viola a hug and fled. As they drove

away in the grey morning light she looked back and saw Viola waving from her window, a forlorn little hand unattached, it seemed, to any face.

'I hope you know what you're doing,' Sebby observed heavily. 'I hope my kitchen is still in one piece when I get back.'

'Viola will soon pick it up,' Katrine insisted.

Cleo yawned. 'You and Viola are very thick lately —she makes a laughable little housewife. I can't think why she bothers. Geoff can afford to pay someone to do it for her.'

Katrine gave her a cool glance. 'It matters to Viola that she should be able to run her own house once she's married. The days of servants and ladies of leisure are over.'

Cleo looked sideways at Sebby, her smile malicious. 'Present company excepted.'

Sebby's thin face grew ferocious. 'I'm not a servant,' he said indignantly. 'So watch your tongue, madam!'

Katrine was astounded. 'Cleo, that was a very nasty thing to say. Sebby's one of the family! Good heavens, I don't think you could have said anything nastier if you'd tried for a hundred years.'

Rolf, dragged from his half-tranced absorption in the traffic, gave Cleo an irate glare. 'I agree! Sheath those claws of yours!'

Sulkily, Cleo lounged back, her lids lowered in a pretence of sleep.

Cantwich was a mellow backwater, sleeping in the Kentish countryside today as it had done for centuries, almost unchanged since the days of Pascal Flint.

There was one long, meandering main street called The High, from which, as from a river, tributaries ran in the shape of winding little alleys crammed with small shops and tiny cottages. Halfway down The High widened out into an irregular square in the centre of which stood a market cross around which the traffic flowed in three directions. There were public houses at regular intervals, with gay signs swinging over their doors; a handful of cafés mainly catering for the tourists and slightly decaying Assembly Room, with a cream-painted portico and elegant Georgian windows.

'My God, it's the back of beyond,' said Cleo, staring about as they drove down the High.

'I think it's charming,' Katrine said gently. 'Do look at the Assembly Rooms, Cleo. Isn't it marvellous? Can't you imagine girls in high-waisted Jane Austen dresses going inside to dance by candlelight with elegant young men? Things were so much more romantic in those days.'

'You're mad,' Cleo said, giving her a disgusted look. 'What's romantic about a time when there was no sanitation to speak of, when the only music was slow and boring, when girls had to have chaperones and were looked on as fast if they enjoyed themselves talking to young men? Give me the twentieth century every time. I like having a good time, thank you!'

'I must say I agree,' Rolf nodded. 'I've never hankered to live in any other time but our own.'

They took a right-hand fork leading out of the town, drove along a hawthorn-bordered lane and turned left at the next junction. The house which Max Neilson had leased for the summer lay half way along a narrow lane. There were no other buildings in sight. A rawboned cob stood in a paddock next to the house, chewing slowly and thoughtfully at the grass. Buttercups and daisies gave a brightness to the unmown field.

The house was clearly of the same general age as the Assembly Rooms, possibly even built by the same architect. A long, stucco front with the usual well proportioned windows, a smaller version of the pillared portico, with a very handsome front door ornamented by a lion's head knocker which gleamed brassily as they arrived.

Rolf hooted, the well-bred little hoot which the Rolls made. Then round the corner of the house strolled Dodie Alexander and Max Neilson, casually dressed in slacks and loose shirts.

'There you are,' Max drawled. 'Come and join us in the garden. We're having tea.'

'We had an early lunch on our way down,' said Rolf. 'I'm starving again. I hope your notion of tea is quite generous.'

'Dodie got it ready,' Max said.

'Sandwiches, cake and ice-cream,' Dodie told them.

Sebby was unpacking the cases. Cleo languidly climbed out of the car and gave Dodie a swift, summing up look. 'Could I see my room? I'm exhausted. Car journeys are so tiring. I need to wash, change.'

'I'll show you,' said Dodie, her amusement thinly veiled. She grinned at Katrine. 'Katya, my darling! I'm happy you are here. Max, take the child and feed her. She is pale.'

He took Katrine's arm. 'Come along, Katya,' he said with irritating mock-solemnity.

'I don't need to be taken,' she said, pulling free. 'I must help Sebby, anyway.'

Sebby, however, was in one of his remote moods. 'I don't need any help, miss,' he said.

'There you are,' Max told her teasingly.

Rolf had already shot off to find the food. Katrine looked uneasily at Sebby. Was he sulking because Cleo had called him a servant? He could take things to heart sometimes. She knew he was touchy on the subject of status.

Max calmly resumed possession of her arm, looking down at her out of those heavy-lidded eyes.

'Do as you're told, child. Sebby doesn't want you at the moment. He's going to prowl about and learn the lie of the land, aren't you, Sebby?'

Sebby had stacked the cases neatly under the portico. He gave Max one of his inscrutable looks.

'That's right, sir.' His tone was bland.

Max grinned at him. 'We'll get out from under your feet, then. Come along, Katya.'

She obeyed reluctantly, and Max gave her a dry smile. 'Look less like an early Christian martyr, my child. I'm beginning to think you don't like me.'

She opened wide, innocent eyes. 'What makes you think that?'

He laughed. 'What, indeed?'

The tea was laid out in the garden, picnic style, on a rough cane table beside which stood two chairs. Rolf sat in one, eating tomato and cucumber sandwiches greedily. He waved to them.

'This lemonade is delicious. Did Dodie make it?'

'No,' said Max, 'I did. My grandmother taught me.' He looked at Katrine, smiling. 'I'll show you some time. You use both lemons and oranges. The orange is to sweeten the juice.' There were wafer-thin slices of orange floating in the green glass jug. Rolf poured a glass for her and Katrine drank thirstily. It was delicious.

Max stretched out on the grass, shading his eyes with one lean hand, while Rolf and Katrine sat at the table eating. There was a blackbird on the chimney, pouring out music, and the sun was hot on Katrine's shoulders. She nibbled at the sandwiches without real relish. For some reason Max's unmoving figure was distracting her mind from other matters. She watched him secretly from beneath lowered lashes. He was long and lean, his shirt collar open at the brown throat, his dark hair ruffled by a slight breeze which blew gently across the grass. Even in repose he commanded attention. She could only see half of his face. His eyes were hidden by the curve of his hand. Below his thin, strong fingers showed that bony nose and the firm, yet mocking mouth, now relaxed in repose. Jaw and cheekbones were tough enough to draw questioning attention to the amusement he so often displayed in his lazy eyes.

Was he really the lazily indifferent man he usually pretended to be?

His features were contradictory, puzzling. Katrine took a small almond cake and bit into it negligently. Rolf pushed back his chair and stood up.

'I'll go and find out what's keeping Cleo and Dodie,' he said.

The silence when he had gone seemed to oppress Katrine's spirits. She decided to follow him, but when she stood up Max opened his eyes and lowered the hand which had shielded his face. 'I want to talk to you,' he said in tones at once light and decisive.

She waited, shifting from one foot to another, like a child about to be reprimanded.

'Sit down here,' Max ordered, patting the grass beside him in a way which brooked no refusal.

She looked at him, flushed and indignant, on the point of refusing, but something about his gaze made her obey. She oddly had the feeling that he had half hoped she *would* refuse—she fancied he had intended some form of reprisal if she did. But when she meekly sat down, he grinned.

'There's a good girl!' The tone was derisory, and she lifted her chin in defiance.

'I ought to go and help Sebby.'

He ignored this faint defiance. 'Why did you stay at home all these years? Why not a career?'

'I didn't want one,' she said.

He raised a quizzical eyebrow. 'No ambition at all? Odd in a Milford.'

'I'm an odd Milford,' she said, hot-cheeked. How dared he question her like this? What right did he think he had?

He studied her oddly. 'So you are,' he murmured. 'Well, your domestic talents will not be needed here. The owner provides a cleaning woman on weekday mornings, and Sebby can do the rest. I've got a different job for you.'

She glared at him. 'Oh, have you? We'll have to consult my father about that.'

'Oh, Rolf has already agreed,' he said easily.

'Well, I haven't,' she said. 'What is this job? Why should I want to work for you?'

'I need an assistant down at the theatre,' he told her calmly. 'To run errands and so on—even you can do that, surely!'

She went pale. 'No,' she said flatly. 'Oh, no.'

His eyes narrowed on her suddenly white face. 'You look as if you're going to faint. What is it?'

'Nothing,' she said, jumping up. 'But I can't work for you, Mr Neilson. I'm sorry. I prefer to continue as I am ...'

He leapt to his feet and tried to catch her hand, but she had already turned in flight, and soon she was out of sight. Max Neilson stood, watching her, his hands now thrust deep into his pockets. A look of odd excitement kindled on his usually remote face. His grey eyes were intently fixed on the house into which Katrine had now vanished.

She had fully expected Sebby's backing, but to her surprise and dismay he was irritatingly complacent about Max Neilson's suggestion.

'Why not? Be fun for you.' He had continued to peer into cupboards, sniffing lugubriously. 'Mould in there, I shouldn't wonder. Needs a good scrub-out with soda.'

'I'll do it,' she offered.

'Later will do,' he shrugged.

'Sebby, I don't want to work down at the theatre,' she said, a little huskily.

'Nothing for you to do here,' he said.

'But you all said there would be a lot of work running this house,' she protested. 'You can't do it all alone.'

He gave her an indignant look. 'Who can't? I'm not helpless, young lady! I could do this standing on my head.'

She helplessly left him prowling about, and went to find her father. However, he was just as bad.

'I think Max is right,' he said jovially. 'An excellent idea. Great fun for you, seeing how we all work, and useful for us to have you around. Always too much work to be done on these rush jobs. Amateurs everywhere, getting under our feet. Enthusiastic souls, of course, but rank amateurs!' He was unpacking his shirts and hanging them in the wardrobe. She took them from him with something of a snatching movement and said, 'Sit down, Fra. I'll do this.'

He watched her complacently. She hung his shirts

up, shaking the faint creases out of them with a practised flick of the wrist. He smiled as she turned back towards him. Oh, yes, she thought triumphantly—he could do without my help! What a silly idea! He can't even hang his shirts up properly.

'There you are,' he said, smiling. 'You can look after my clothes in the theatre.'

'Why do you and Max want me down there, Fra?' she asked him point blank.

Rolf looked rather evasively at her. 'Don't we always want you around, darling?' He started to pull ties out of his case. She took them and began to hang them up, too.

Clearly she was not going to get any answers from her father. Indeed, she knew very well that she must go to Max for an answer. This she was reluctant to do, for reasons she preferred not to think about.

Over supper Rolf eagerly questioned Max about the production. He had once met Pascal Flint, when he was a boy and the old playwright was already a myth in his own lifetime. 'I saw this play when I was ten years old,' he confided to Max. 'Flint was present. He sat in the front row, growling like a bear with a sore head. Drunken old reprobate!'

Max told him that the cast were very young, very enthusiastic. 'They'll work like mad,' he nodded. 'Although they're so young they've all had experience. Professionals to their fingertips.'

Rolf was undisturbed by the news that the cast were so young. His golden confidence was unbroken. Katrine, watching him, was moved to see how little he felt the passing of the years, how much he relied upon his own untapped reserves of energy. He leaned back in his chair, relaxed and smiling, wearing a sort of radiance in his still handsome face. In his twenties he had been the toast of London, a matinee idol, regarded by the critics as a young actor of great promise but by his female audiences as a golden heart-throb.

That dazzling beauty had passed long since. He had matured into a distinguished, attractive man. On stage, in make-up, he was still at a distance handsome enough to stop the heart.

'Tomorrow we'll drive down to the theatre,' Max told him.

'Good,' Rolf beamed, satisfied both by this news and by the meal he had just consumed with every evidence of enjoyment. 'I think I shall enjoy this country living, my boy. Peace, quiet, good food ... When do rehearsals start?'

Max grinned. 'The sooner the peace stops the better, eh? Well, I thought we would have a casual chat together in the theatre bar tomorrow. I called the whole cast for ten o'clock. We'll discuss things for an hour, then have a break for drinks.'

Rolf laughed. 'That's what I call a splendid scheme. You're a director after my own heart, Max.' He gave him a thoughtful look. 'We're using an uncut text, I hope?'

Max eyed him wryly. 'That's a subject we'll discuss tomorrow, Rolf. No shop talk now.' He glanced at Katrine. 'You can drive down with us, Katya.'

Dodie, who had been silent during the talk so far, looked up. Cleo opened her huge eyes in astonishment.

'Katrine?' she asked, her inflection incredulous.

Rolf looked vague. 'Yes, I've decided she can make herself useful down at the theatre.'

'You've decided,' Cleo drawled, eyeing Max inquisitively.

He gave her one of his bland smiles. 'Your father thinks Katrine spends too much time shut up at home. She ought to find out what being a Milford means.'

'Fra must have changed his mind lately,' Cleo observed. 'He always said Katrine wasn't meant for the stage.'

Rolf restlessly moved away. 'I can change my mind, I suppose, can't I?' He looked at Dodie imploringly. 'How about a game of chess?'

She smiled encouragingly at him, her great dark eyes warm. 'That would be very enjoyable, darling.'

'What are you up to, Max?' Cleo asked him, when her father and Dodie had gone.

He looked mildly at her. 'I don't understand. Why should I be up to anything?'

Cleo was not to be shaken off. 'You know quite well that Fra has always been happy to keep Katrine at home. Why should he suddenly want her to get involved in show business? It is either your idea or ...' She stared at the door with narrowed eyes. 'Or ...'

'Or what?' Max asked softly.

'Or dear, darling Dodie's,' said Cleo, her lips thinning. 'But why should Dodie Alexander take such a close interest in my little sister?'

'Dodie is very fond of Katya,' said Max.

'Don't call her that!' Cleo snapped.

Katrine, who had been silent throughout this exchange, looked up in baffled surprise at the sudden sharpness of Cleo's voice. Cleo, catching the expression on her sister's expressive little face, grinned ruefully.

'I'm a bit on edge,' she explained. 'Max, do you think I can handle this part?'

He gave a faintly amused look to her. 'You can do it on your head, my girl,' he said gently. 'Why else do you think I asked you to do it?'

'I'm not too certain about her character,' Cleo sighed. 'Is she really a bitch, or am I imagining it? Is she meant to be tough on the outside, but with a heart of gold?'

'We can discuss all that in rehearsals,' said Max. 'You know my methods, Watson. I like to have a free-for-all discussion about the play before we get down to close analysis of each individual character. A play is a unit. Each character is a thread woven into the general pattern of the cloth.'

'How intellectual you are, darling,' Cleo murmured, stretching her arms above her head in a smothered yawn. She was wearing a simple white tunic which perfectly offset her golden tan and the red-gold hair which fell around her lovely face. As she moved the jersey silk stretched, outlining her slender body. Max's eyes admired the movement openly, a little smile on his mouth.

Cleo smiled back, well satisfied by the look he had given her. 'It's a gorgeous evening. I'm eager to stroll around the garden. Coming?'

'Why not?' Max stood up, took her extended hand and pulled her to her feet in a jerk which brought her close to him, her eyes gazing into his.

Katrine went out to Sebby, indignant. 'Everyone is determined to make me work down at the theatre!'

'I don't know what your objection is,' Sebby grunted. 'Most girls of your age would love to spend a few weeks working with great stars of the theatre.'

Katrine bit her lip. 'I'm not most girls.'

'What's your objection?' Sebby asked, point blank.

'Do you think I want to hang around there, having everyone look at me in disbelief when they find out I'm a Milford, one of the Magnificent Milfords, the beautiful Milfords?' She was dark red, her eyes blazing. 'All my life I've been forced to see myself in other people's eyes, see their faces when they hear my name. I'm plain—worse still, I have no talents. I'm a disappointment to my father and an embarrassment to my sisters. Now, for some whim of Max Neilson's, my father is trying to make me go through all that again, when I'd made a niche for myself at home.' She ended up on a gasp which was half a sob.

Sebby handed her a tea towel, patted her gently on the shoulder. 'Come, no tears! Dry your eyes and then dry up the supper things. I'll speak to Max Neilson.'

'You won't tell him what I've just said?' she begged.

'Of course not,' Sebby rebuked her.

The door opened and Dodie Alexander came in, laughing. She gave them both a warm look of pleasure. 'How nice it is to have you here, Katya love.'

Sebby hurried to pull out a kitchen chair for her, plumping up a patchwork cushion for her back. 'Madame ...' he invited with a ceremonious half wave, half bow.

She sat down, graceful as a queen, smiling up at him. 'Oh, Sebby, I have come in search of coffee ... I have just allowed Rolf to beat me at chess, and the exertion of not winning has quite dehydrated me!'

Sebby hurried to make fresh coffee, delighted to do something for his goddess. Ever since Katrine could remember, Sebby had been Dodie's devoted slave. It was something of a family joke, kindly meant, for they were all fond of both Sebby and Dodie.

The kitchen was capacious, stone-flagged, with a very old cottage-style door with an old iron latch. It had been modernised, recently, and had all the desired conveniences of the time, even to a deep-freezer and a dishwasher, but Sebby had no faith in the latter machine, since he liked to wash good china by hand and was quite superstitiously afraid that the machine might break his precious bone china.

Floral chintz hung at the window, a dark Welsh

dresser stood in a corner and Sebby had already arranged some yellow roses in a green glass vase for the kitchen table.

Dodie patted the chair beside her. 'Come and talk to me, Katya.'

Katrine obeyed, smilingly. Dodie always exuded a delightful perfume, the familiar scent she had always worn since Katrine could remember. It was light, summery, intimate. In its gaiety and sweetness it was typical of Dodie herself. Looking at her, Katrine felt a great affection for her.

'Your father tells me you do not want to come to the theatre to watch us at work,' Dodie said softly.

Katrine felt herself flush. 'No,' she said huskily.

'Why not, my dear?' Dodie's dark eyes searched hers.

Katrine swallowed. 'I ... I'm not happy when I'm in the theatre,' she almost whispered.

Dodie nodded, almost as if it was the answer she had expected. 'You feel you do not belong there?' she asked.

Katrine nodded. 'Yes ... yes, that's it.'

'Why is that, do you think?' Dodie asked, very gently, still watching the girl intently.

'I don't know.'

'Are you sure?' Dodie put a hand on Katrine's, patting it. 'I think I might be able to guess, my dear.' She spoke softly, lovingly. 'You are too sensitive about the fact that you are not as lovely as your two sisters, that you do not have their confidence and ability to over-awe young men on first sight.

Beauty is not necessarily the passport to achievement, you know. All actresses are not raving beauties.' She laughed wryly. 'I am no beauty myself.'

'Oh, you,' said Katrine, shrugging.

Dodie laughed again. 'What does that mean, that face?'

'You're a superb actress,' Katrine said shyly. 'You know you are. You didn't need to be beautiful.'

Quietly, Dodie asked, 'Did you feel you needed to be beautiful, my Katya?'

Katrine went pink, did not answer.

'When you were small, did you suffer much from your lack of beauty?' Dodie probed very gently, watching her all the time. 'Did you feel rejected, a failure, because you were not one of the golden Milfords?'

'Fra called me a changeling,' Katrine burst out revealingly.

'Ah,' sighed Dodie. 'Your father has always said more than he meant.'

Sebby brought them both coffee, discreetly withdrew again, a watchful listening presence in the background.

'You will talk to Fra,' begged Katrine. 'Persuade him to give up this idea? I'm sure it was Max Neilson's idea in the first place. It would be just like him—interfering beast!'

Dodie gave her a secretive look. 'I tell you what I will do,' she murmured. 'I will take you into Great Graceham tomorrow—there is a fascinating little boutique there. I found it last week. The woman who runs it makes the clothes herself, or designs them and has them made on the premises, I forget which. She has some extraordinary models in stock. You're a thin little thing, you must be stock size. We'll see what we can do with you. All you need is to be taken in hand.'

Katrine was bewildered. 'But you will talk to Fra and Max Neilson?'

Dodie patted her cheek. 'Will you promise me to be patient? Tomorrow afternoon, after lunch, I'll take you to the boutique. But in the morning you must come down to the theatre, as Rolf wants it. In the evening, we'll talk to your father together. How's that?'

Katrine hesitated, then said, 'Oh, yes, I suppose that will do.'

'Then smile,' Dodie teased.

Katrine managed a little smile and was given a kiss as a reward. Sebby beamed upon her approvingly and refilled their coffee cups.

CHAPTER FOUR

THE Cantwich Theatre had once been a corn mill. It stood beside the River Durdle among newly laid down lawns. Whitewashed, simple and functional it had a peculiar, unique charm. The Festival Committee had turned the old mill into a theatre because it was a way of killing two birds with one stone. The mill had had a preservation order imposed upon it, and the idea of the Festival had been mooted at the same time, and some great brain had come up with the idea of dealing with both problems in one move.

The exterior had been left almost untouched, apart from necessary repair work and painting. Inside, however, it was a different story.

They had reduced the interior to a shell, then built a 'thrust' stage so that the actors could move out among the audience on the raised level. The seats were built around the stage in a semi-circle. It was a small, intimate little theatre so designed that it could be used for a multitude of purposes from amateur dramatics to pop concerts.

A small restaurant had been built beside the Mill Theatre. The building was carefully designed to match its surroundings. The inevitable car park spoiled some of the charm of the area, to Katrine's way of thinking, but she supposed it was inescapable in these motor-car-orientated days.

Max drove them down. Rolf had already taken Dodie in his Rolls, leaving Katrine and Cleo to accompany Max.

Cleo wore thin white cotton jeans and sleeveless top. She looked cool, elegant and casual. Katrine wore a neat navy blue skirt with a white shirt blouse. Beside her beautiful sister she looked like a schoolgirl, and Max's mocking gaze told her as much.

The theatre bar was attached to the restaurant. It

ran in a half-moon along the riverside, the windows looking out upon the cool green waters.

The bar was crowded with young men and girls in jeans. They all stopped talking as Rolf, Dodie and the others made their entrance. Rolf and Dodie had stopped en route to pick up a parcel from the railway station. Dodie had been expecting some shoes from London for days and they had just arrived in time for the first rehearsal. Dodie had a passion for expensive footwear. Her tiny, elegant feet were never crammed into ordinary factory manufactured shoes. She had her shoes hand-made in London at incredible prices.

The newcomers paused, instinctively, while the rest of the cast looked at them.

Rolf switched on his most charming smile. He glanced around the young crowd. 'Good morning, everyone! So sorry we're late! Bad form, being late for first rehearsal.' He looked penitent, as if he might at any moment assume sackcloth and ashes. Everyone laughed and murmured deprecatingly.

Max took Katrine's arm. 'Stay with me. I may need you.' He pushed his way through the crowd and pulled himself up on the bar so that everyone could see him.

'Good morning, everyone!' He looked round their upturned faces. 'Are we all here?' He glanced down at Katrine. 'Will you count them?' he asked her in businesslike tones.

She climbed up on the bar too and carefully counted heads. Among them she recognised Nicky.

He looked at her in surprise and winked. She blushed.

'Twenty-five,' she whispered to Max.

'Good. Everybody's here.' He handed her a typed list. 'Go round now and check the names off on this list. Try to memorise their faces so that you'll know them next time you see them.'

She slid down and obediently began to check the list. Some of the faces were already well known. She exchanged light courtesies and nods here and there. When she came to Nicky he looked at her from under his thick light lashes.

'Hello, sweetie. Since when were you Max Neilson's secretary?'

'Since this morning,' she said lightly.

'Rather you than me. He can be a bastard.' Nicky spoke with unusual vehemence.

'You don't like him?' She sounded more surprised than she was, considering her own opinion of Max.

'Does anyone except Dodie Alexander? Is it true that they plan to get married while they're down here?'

Katrine shrugged. 'How should I know? I'm not in their confidence.'

Nicky nodded. 'Your opinion of Max Neilson was always pretty low, I seem to recall, but you liked Dodie.'

'I still do,' she agreed. 'Dodie is kindness itself, especially to young actors. She always tries to put them at their ease.' She glanced across the room at where Dodie stood, surrounded by an eager crowd of young people all competing for her attention. Dodie looked tenderly amused, listening with an unfeigned interest to their excited talk about the production in rehearsal. Although she had been at the top for so long, Dodie retained an enormous enthusiasm and zest for her profession. Shop talk was as fascinating to her now as it was to these young beginners on the ladder of success.

Nicky's gaze followed Katrine's, and at that moment a girl turned and looked at them briefly. She was pretty; tall with long chestnut hair and hazel eyes. Her skin was glowingly healthy.

Noticing the resentment in those hazel eyes, Katrine looked up at Nicky inquiringly.

He grimaced at her, half shrugging, with a look of wry self-mockery.

'Problems, Nicky?' Katrine asked huskily. She could guess why the other girl was glaring at them.

'Pauline is playing Mary-Ann in *Hazard Green*,' Nicky lamely explained. 'I've been seeing a bit of her—you know how it is.'

'I know,' Katrine said. She moved on with a polite nod. She had to get away before Nicky saw the pain in her face. There was no earthly reason why Nicky shouldn't take another girl out. There had never been anything other than light flirtation between them, and Nicky had made her no promises. For her own self-respect she must hide how much it hurt.

When she returned to Max he took the list, glanced down and nodded. The heavy-lidded eyes were alarmingly perceptive. She looked away from their probing intelligence.

He already knew far too much about her, she thought. She thoroughly disliked men of his kidney—arrogant, interfering, omniscient men who brooked no clash with their view of their own authority.

Everyone found a seat. Some of the girls curled up on the wooden parquet floor, like kittens, bright-eyed and curious. Some of the young men perched on the bar. Max leaned against a chair and looked round at their faces, his eyes intent.

He talked to them coolly about Pascal Flint's life and work, his place in the English theatre, his place in world theatre.

'We're going to attract tourists from all over the world. This production has got to be first-class. I want no unprofessional behaviour, no lightweights. We're here to work, to learn, to extend ourselves...'

Katrine was looking at the charcoal sketch of the playwright hanging over the bar. She recognised it easily enough. It had been done by Augustus John. A few swift strokes and a strong, dominant personality looked out at you from the white page. Pascal Flint had not been an easy man to know. He had been wild, unpredictable and impossible for his friends. But he had been a genius, too, and it was the genius who had been captured in this sketch. There was rough power in the tilt of the head, the line of the mouth.

Max went on to talk about the two plays which

had been the basis for Flint's lasting acclaim.

Katrine heard him talking about *Button Man*, heard him pause to ask her father something, heard her father humbly answer, with a suitably modest smile.

Max listened gravely. The young faces looked at the great Rolf Milford and were impressed by his sincerity.

Max turned and looked down at Katrine. His bony nose and lazy eyes were expressionless, yet she discerned a sardonic amusement hidden somewhere behind the mask of his features.

Anyone who really knew Rolf would have been amused to see him playing to the gallery like this.

Later, as they drove back to the house, Max murmured to her, 'Rolf assumes a virtue though he has it not...' misquoting wittily with a slight smile.

The first rehearsal had been a social occasion, 'a talk-in', as Max had called it, designed chiefly to weld the two diverse elements of the casts together —the famous stars, trailing their clouds of glory, with the eager young unknowns who were to form the sound repertory base for the season.

It had been necessary to make it clear that hard work was to be the order of the day for everyone.

'He's a tartar,' someone had said happily as they left. They had been left under no illusions. Max was going to drive them hard.

He had invited discussions on the texts, assured them all that he believed in full participation by the cast, yet for all that he had listened seriously to what even the newest member of the cast had to say, there had never been in their minds a doubt as to who would be the arbiter in any argument. Max's authority rested upon his own personality. His cool, immovable voice commanded instant attention.

I loathe and detest him, Katrine thought resentfully. For her the morning had been humiliating. She had lost count of the number of times she had been made aware of her complete contrast to her sisters—not once but half a dozen times someone had said, 'You're one of the Milfords?' And the incredulity had stung. Her mirror had told her from her earliest years what those voices had underlined. She was thin, pale and dark—a changeling in the golden Milford family, a natural outsider.

I will not go down there again, she decided grimly. When they got back Sebby was waiting, lunch exactly and perfectly timed for their arrival. He had made Rolf's favourite consommé, followed by steak and salad, followed by strawberry meringue and cream. Over lunch everyone talked. Katrine nibbled at her food, pushing her steak about with a faint grimace of distaste. She was not a bit hungry.

'We'll leave for the boutique in an hour,' Dodie told her as they drank their coffee. 'I must take my nap first.' She smiled wryly. 'I am getting old and I need a regular pattern of sleep.'

Rolf looked at her placidly. 'Darling Dodie, if you are getting old, I must be in my dotage.'

'Max darling,' drawled Cleo, 'come and sunbathe in the garden with me ...'

'Later,' Max told her. 'I want a word with your sister first.'

Cleo looked from him to Katrine. 'Very well,' she said, tossing back her red-gold hair with a petulant little gesture.

Katrine went into the kitchen to see if Sebby needed any help, but he had already washed up and vanished. He had become rather remote since they arrived. Katrine suspected Sebby of communing with nature. He was a Londoner by conviction as well as by circumstance, but every now and then he grew sentimental about the countryside and enjoyed a few hours of peace away from town. It never lasted long. Like most infatuations it was violent, but brief.

Max followed her into the room and stood in the doorway, looking irritatingly reposed as he leaned in the angle of door and wall.

'So did your morning in the theatre fulfil all your worst expectations?' he asked sardonically.

She mutinously refused to reply, her face locked against his probing eyes. He should not see how bitterly she resented her position in the family. Her instinct was to lick her wounds in privacy, and Max was the last person she wanted to observe her at this moment.

'You stubborn little idiot,' he said, suddenly, on a very uncharacteristic note of infuriated warmth. 'Hasn't anyone ever told you what a superb voice you've got locked away in that throat of yours?'

She turned, pink and startled. 'What?' He had taken her utterly by surprise.

He laughed at her expression of disbelief and bewilderment. 'My good girl, I can see you've never heard yourself! Come upstairs with me ...'

She stood, rooted to the spot. 'Why?'

'I am not planning seduction in my bedroom, if that's what's in that suspicious little head of yours,' he retorted irritably. 'I have a tape recorder upstairs.'

She looked at him incredulously. 'You want to make a recording of me?'

He was silent, nodding at her. Katrine swallowed. He was quite serious! After a moment, she said stammeringly, 'No, I couldn't ... Anyway, I've got to go to this boutique with Dodie.'

Dodie appeared behind Max, smiled at them both impartially, in a motherly way. 'I was too excited to sleep for long. My mental discipline is obviously slipping! But I might as well use the time. Are you ready, Katya my dear?'

Relieved, Katrine nodded. Max stood aside, grim and faintly mocking. 'The subject is only shelved, Katya my dear,' he drawled in pointed mimicry. 'I'll come back to it later.'

She gave him a hunted glance and fled.

Dodie was curious, but tactful. 'You and Max have a strange relationship,' she hinted gently, as they drove through the peaceful ountryside. 'He is a genius, in his way, you know.'

'He has all the makings of a petty dictator,' said Katrine with bitter emphasis.

Dodie laughed gently. 'Be careful, my dear. Max

is quite ruthless. He always gets what he wants.'

For some reason which Katrine dared not analyse, this remark brought a bright flush to her face. Dodie laughed again, but made no other comment.

The boutique was located in a back street, but the unprepossessing exterior was misleading. Only one dress was arranged in the tiny window, a striped black and white evening dress with a high, frilled neckline at the front giving a demure appearance very much belied by the plunging back, cut to the waist in a dramatic scoop.

The woman who owned the shop served them. Dodie and she conferred discreetly, eyeing Katrine in a way which made her very nervous.

Soon she found herself being pushed into dress after dress. Dodie and the proprietor stared at her from every angle, nodding or frowning, exclaiming or groaning.

Dodie finally decided upon two dresses, both vivid, dramatic garments quite unlike anything Katrine ever bought herself. One was a warm apricot jersey silk, clinging and elegant, with a loose swathed neckline. The other was vivid green, full-skirted and tight-waisted, with a charming, scalloped bodice. Dodie also made her buy a trouser suit, in crisp linen, the colour of cinnamon, with darker piping.

'And that dress in the window,' Dodie added finally. 'Could we have that out? It looks as if it would fit her.'

'Oh, it will,' agreed the proprietor eagerly. 'And

if I may say so, it will suit her very well.'

'I couldn't!' cried Katrine in horror.

Dodie was determined. 'Yes,' she nodded to the other woman. 'Definitely.'

They ignored Katrine's protests. She was somehow persuaded to try the dress on, and when she saw herself from the front she was pacified to some extent, but her back view startled her into another moan of alarm. 'It's much too low ...'

Dodie laughed. 'My dear Katya, you are almost entirely covered from head to foot. At the front.'

'But the back ...'

'Enchanting,' Dodie nodded.

'Perfect,' agreed the other woman.

Katya looked at them in despair. 'I would never have the sheer nerve to be seen in it,' she announced.

'You will wear it to the first night of *Button Man*,' Dodie told her cheerfully. 'We shall see you in a new light.'

'I don't want to be seen in a new light,' Katrine stammered miserably.

They laughed in unison, as if she had said something terribly funny. Katrine did not laugh. She was wondering what her father would say when he saw the bills for these clothes. She had just, incredulously, caught sight of the ticket on the trouser suit, and the figure made her feel weak at the knees. While the proprietor was off looking for boxes in which to pack the clothes, she hectically whispered to Dodie her views on the price of the dresses.

'Never mind the cost,' Dodie said easily. 'I have arranged it with Rolf.'

'But I've never paid these sort of prices for my clothes,' said Katrine unhappily.

'That is the trouble,' Dodie murmured. 'Why else do you think you look like a schoolgirl? Because you buy such appalling clothes! You are a Milford. It is time you dressed like one.'

'I wear jeans most of the time,' Katrine said. 'I like wearing jeans.'

'Jeans!' Dodie laughed. 'Why not? For the occasions when jeans are appropriate! But what of cocktail parties, dinner parties and first nights? Then you look like a refugee from a Girl Guide camp! You need warmth, colour, grace, and I have made sure that in future you will have them.'

When they got back to the house they found everyone lying in the garden in attitudes of complete relaxation. Cleo was wearing a silver bikini, dark glasses and a floppy straw hat in a very becoming shade of blue.

Max, in cotton slacks and a short-sleeved cotton top, was apparently asleep in a deck chair. Rolf was reading his copy of *Button Man*, his lips moving silently as he read. From time to time his face would twist in silent emphasis as he registered some emotion.

Dodie looked at them all with tender amusement. 'Lazybones, all of you,' she said.

Max opened his eyes. He took in Katrine, nervously aware of the new green dress she was wearing. An odd glint came into his heavy-lidded eyes.

'Well, well, well,' he drawled.

Cleo sat up, taking off her sun-glasses. Her eyes widened. 'What's been going on? Who's the Fairy Godmother, or need I ask?' She glanced at Dodie, smiling too sweetly. 'Been waving your magic wand, have you, Dodie dear?'

Dodie looked amused, as if the children were misbehaving. 'Now, now,' she said tolerantly. 'You surely are not jealous of your little sister, Cleo my love?'

Cleo laughed coldly. 'Of Katrine?' Her tone was icily contemptuous.

Max had not taken his eyes off Katrine. His glance roved deliberately, coolly, from her head to her feet.

Dodie had whisked her off to a hairdresser. Her dark brown hair had been shaped elegantly around her thin face, revealing the delicacy of her bone structure, the enormous width of her dark blue eyes. She wore little make-up, but her eyes had been emphasised by a blue eyeshadow and a layer of false eyelashes. They had found time to buy her new shoes, too—Dodie's obsession with feet making her regard good shoes as no luxury but a necessity. Katrine was deeply pleased with her shoes—they were tiny, elegant green leather.

Max gave Dodie a quick, approving smile. 'You've worked a small miracle.'

Dodie laughed. 'It took great persistence. The victim struggled every inch of the way.'

Max grinned. 'I can imagine.'

Cleo stared suspiciously from one to the other. 'I smell a conspiracy. Is this do-good-to-Katrine week, by any chance?'

Max flickered her a faint smile. 'Miaow!'

Katrine flushed. 'I don't need charity, thank you!' She turned and went into the house. Cleo laughed. Dodie looked at her with cool appraisal.

'What a jealous little cat you are,' she said softly. 'How uncertain and unhappy you must be if you find it necessary to be so cruel to your sister. I am quite sorry for you.'

Cleo flushed angrily. 'Sorry for me? It's Katrine you should be sorry for. She's been perfectly happy running the house, but you two will make her discontented if you go on with this Fairy Godmother stunt. Very kind and generous of you, no doubt, but I'm afraid misguided.' She sauntered into the house, her head held high.

Rolf looked at Max and Dodie thoughtfully. 'What's wrong with Cleo? She's a beautiful girl, yet she is always so difficult...'

'Perhaps she believes her own publicity,' Max murmured. 'She has come up rather fast. Stardom is sometimes a problem if you reach it too soon. Cleo isn't very old. I wonder if she finds fame a bitter pleasure?'

Dodie nodded. 'Certainly she has a hectic look sometimes. It does happen that one loses one's balance at times. The glare of publicity dazzles one. Blinds one, even.'

'Do you think so?' Rolf looked bewildered. 'I never found it so.'

Max and Dodie laughed. 'Dearest Rolf,' murmured Dodie, bending to kiss him on the cheek. 'How very uncomplicated you are at times! So relaxing.'

Rolf looked pleased but still puzzled. Max sauntered after them as they went indoors to change before tea. Sebby was busy in the kitchen when Katrine came to join him. He had prepared a plate of minute, triangular sandwiches; some iced fairy cakes, some chocolate marzipan slices (for Rolf who adored them) and an elaborate confection of jelly and whipped cream.

Katrine was safely back in jeans. She felt as if she had slipped back into invisibility. Something about Max's prolonged gaze had made her stomach twist nervously.

'What's all this about new clothes?' asked Sebby, staring at her. 'Your hair looks nice. Suits you.'

'Thank you,' she said. 'What can I do to help?'

'Carry this tray out to the garden,' said Sebby. 'Where are these new clothes?'

'Upstairs,' she said flatly.

'When are we going to see them, then?'

'Yes,' Max murmured sardonically from the door. 'When? I see you're back in jeans. Retreating in panic, Katya? It won't do you any good.'

She looked at him with a sudden feeling of sheer hatred, as if she felt he was entirely to blame for all the vague unhappiness and discontent which was bedevilling her lately. 'Oh, why don't you mind your own business?'

CHAPTER FIVE

AT her father's insistence, Katrine wore her new trouser suit next morning at the second rehearsal. Cleo's eyes narrowed when she saw it, but whatever she had been about to say withered on her lips. She herself wore lime green, another of her simple yet devastating tunics, sleeveless and brief-skirted, showing off her golden-brown legs.

'Very efficient this morning, aren't we?' Max murmured to Katrine as they all gathered in the theatre bar for a reading of the complete text. She had provided him with a pad and pencil, a stopwatch and his copy of the play.

She looked demurely down at her hands without answering. She had decided to use a low profile technique in her running battle with Max. Head-on collision only ended in her defeat. He was too clever for her in verbal argument. She would see how discretion would answer.

Nicky was the last to arrive, sauntering in, his golden head sleekly brushed, his handsome features tanned. He threw Max a smile. 'Sorry, old thing. I overslept.'

'When I call rehearsal for a certain hour I expect

everyone to be on time,' Max said coldly. 'Everyone. Understood?'

'Oh, of course,' Nicky said winningly, still smiling.

They launched into the text without much of a preamble from Max. The reading was fast, casual, without expression. They were just finding out the general outlines of the plot for the moment.

When they broke up, Nicky approached Katrine, his blue eyes surprised by admiration. 'You look fantastic! What have you done to yourself? That suit is very becoming. Have lunch with me?'

She laughed, growing pink. 'Thank you.' It was an invitation which made her heartbeat quicken, made her suddenly conscious of her hands and feet, her awkwardness in movement. She so much wanted to look elegant and graceful for Nicky, yet her very self-awareness seemed to increase her clumsiness.

Max turned calmly. 'Sorry. I need you during the lunch hour today. Rehearsals re-commence at two, by the way, Nicky, so don't be late again, will you?'

Nicky gave a charming shrug. He smiled at Katrine. 'A pity. Some other time, perhaps.' Then, to Max, 'I'll be punctual, don't worry.'

'For your own sake I hope you mean that,' said Max. He turned and looked at Katrine, his heavy-lidded eyes taking in the angry expression on her face. 'I'm afraid it will be a working lunch for us. I've some notes I want to dictate to you.'

'I don't know shorthand,' she said, rather pleased to be able to thwart him.

'I'll still need you. You type, don't you? I've seen you typing at home.'

She admitted reluctantly that she could type, and Max said he would dictate and she could type the notes out instead of taking them down in shorthand first.

The theatre restaurant provided them with sandwiches, fruit and coffee. They ate and drank as Max dictated. He stalked to and fro, a frown on his face, rapidly talking about the production. Ideas for lighting, costume and movement spilled out. Katrine began by feeling sulky. She had wanted badly to lunch with Nicky. But as time went on she was dragged reluctantly into fascinated involvement with Max's ideas. It was a dazzling display. He was like a juggler keeping a dozen different coloured balls in the air, his hands moving so fast they blurred. Katrine watched him with faint awe. How could one man be so clever, so inventive and alert? He saw everything, missed nothing.

She was beginning to fear him as much as she had always disliked him. He was too all-seeing.

The natural instinct of humanity to hide, to seek privacy in emotional turmoil, made Max her enemy. Like Eve in the Garden of Eden she felt naked beneath the omniscient eye.

Suddenly he flung her a book of poems. 'Find me that sonnet Flint wrote to his French mistress,' he ordered sharply as he turned on his heel and strode out of the room.

He was back in a moment, just as she found the

poem. She offered him the book, open at the page. He went towards her, hand outstretched. The telephone rang. Max picked it up. 'Hello? Yes, Neilson here. Oh, fine. I'll hold ...' He looked at Katrine with lifted brows. 'Read the poem aloud,' he commanded.

His cool tone was so confident that she had begun to read before he realised it. She had insensibly picked up a certain degree of professionalism in reading aloud. The sonnet was one she knew quite well and found very moving. She was on the last line when Max lifted a hand to silence her, then spoke into the receiver. 'Did you have your lunch? Fine, then come in here.'

The door opened behind Katrine and Dodie came in smiling. Max pulled out a chair for her. 'Sit here and listen.' He pulled out the top drawer of his desk and Katrine, with disbelief and horror, saw a tape recorder, still working. Max stopped it, grinned at her across the room.

'Are you sitting comfortably? Then we'll begin.' He fiddled with the black machine for a moment. A whirring sound as he adjusted the tape, then her own voice filled the room.

Hot colour filled her cheeks. She glared at him, hating him. The sound of her own voice made her writhe in dismay and shame. She would have run out of the room had not Dodie reached across and taken her hand comfortingly, patting her with gentle, warm affection.

As the final words died away Max clicked the

machine off and looked at Dodie, his eyes gleaming oddly.

Katrine leapt to her feet. 'I suppose you think that's funny,' she snapped. 'Tricking me like that! You never consider other people. Well, now you've heard how ghastly I sound maybe you'll leave me alone in future. I've told you—I hate the theatre. I don't want anything to do with it. I have no talent, no ambition. Just leave me alone!'

Max moved very agilely as she fled towards the door. His long arm shot out and arrested her, his fingers seizing her wrist, holding her back.

'Silly, maddening little fool,' he grinned.

Dodie rose and smiled at her. 'My darling Katya, you must be deaf! Your voice is lovely, extraordinarily expressive. I cannot think why nobody has noticed it before. Your family are all deaf too, I must imagine!'

Katrine stood very still, her wrist still held by Max, looking at Dodie incredulously. 'My voice ... lovely?' She swallowed. 'Dodie, I heard it, too, remember. It was dreadful. Squeaky at one moment and hoarse the next.'

Max laughed. She glared at him.

'But, dearest,' Dodie said with affectionate amusement, 'you have an incredible range. That is why your voice is so expressive.'

'It swoops upwards like a swallow, then sinks to a husky, tragic whisper,' Max said to Dodie, looking at her with a smile in his eyes that made Katrine blink. Surely the gossip about these two must be true. Max Neilson would only look like that at a woman he loved. She had never imagined he could look so tender, so caressingly aware of anyone. Was Dodie in love with him, in her turn? Katrine could not be certain.

Dodie was nodding, smiling happily. 'Max, what are we going to do with this blind little angel of ours?'

'Teach her how to use her wings,' Max said calmly.

'How many more times must I tell you,' cried Katrine hectically, 'I'm quite happy as I am!'

'You're a coward,' Max said contemptuously. 'You're so afraid to fall that you won't climb an inch.' He looked down into her uplifted face with a menacing smile. 'Cowards have to learn that it's easier to fight than to run away because no matter how fast you run fate can run faster.'

She pulled at her wrist, struggling to free herself. Max coolly tightened his grip, smiling down at her vain fury.

'You big bully,' she spat bitterly. 'Let me go!'

'I never relinquish anything,' Max drawled.

Dodie clicked her tongue disapprovingly. 'Max darling, let the child go! You are behaving very autocratically this morning!'

'He's a natural tyrant,' Katrine flung at him.

He let go of her and she rubbed her wrist resentfully. Dodie frowned at him. 'I cannot think what has got into you, Max. It is not like you.' She turned towards Katrine, her great dark eyes loving. 'But, my darling, Max is right in what he says about you. You have a voice which it would be a crime to leave unused. God gave you that voice for one purpose—it is a talent to be used. You must use it.'

'Acting needs more than a voice,' Katrine said despairingly.

Dodie nodded. 'Oh, of course. It needs stage presence, personality ...'

'Which I do not possess,' said Katrine.

'You've never stepped on to a stage,' Max said scornfully.

'I know I haven't got it, though,' she retorted.

Max laughed, lifting wry brows. 'Just as you knew your voice was ghastly?'

'Oh!' she seethed helplessly.

He stood there, his eyes lazily mocking her. 'Why should we lie to you? You have a great deal more to offer than your voice, believe me. Your face is striking, even if you're not one of the chocolate-box Milfords!'

She gasped. 'Chocolate-box!'

'Of course they are, those healthy animals of your family—all blonde hair and sex appeal.' He tapped his forehead. 'They have nothing up here.' He tapped his chest. 'Or in here! Neither sensitivity nor intellect. Rolf acts with his instincts, and for him those instincts work pretty well. Viola has always been frivolous. Funny, even witty at times, but she can't move an audience to tears. Cleo ... well, Cleo is a knockout. She walks on a stage and every man in the audience falls in love with her. But act? She can't act for toffee.'

Katrine was dumbfounded, groping for her wits. She couldn't believe her ears. All the temples of her youth were crashing around her. Was it really Max Neilson saying these unbelievable things? She had grown up with the knowledge that every member of her family except herself was brilliant, talented, beautiful. Now Max was bringing the world toppling about her.

Dodie slid an arm around her, stroked her cheek. 'The child is bewildered, Max. You should not say these things to her. She is loyal to her family.'

'It's time she saw them as they really are,' he said impatiently. 'They're successful at projecting themselves—don't you see, Katya? They're the beautiful people, the jet-set, the golden Milfords. But there's more than one mould. Few actors today follow the Milford pattern, and most of us would think that that's an improvement. Actors today need to work hard, think clearly, feel strongly—not just look pretty! Take a look at the company I've gathered for this Festival. They're young, tough, enthusiastic. You won't see their faces in the fashion magazines or television advertisements. They're not fashionable jet-setters. They're workers with a tough job to do and the brains to do it.'

'If you despise my family so much, why have you asked Rolf and Cleo to appear at your precious Festival?' She glared at him with scornful dislike. He criticised her family, yet used them shamelessly.

Max shrugged. 'Rolf, beneath the surface gloss, is perfectly aware of his own capacities and uses them to the utmost. That is all life asks of us—that we use our talents to the full. It doesn't matter what you do so much as that you extend yourself to the limit of your own capacity.'

Dodie was nodding with a serious expression, patting Katrine's hand. 'Max is right, darling.'

'You aren't extended to your limit,' he went on bitingly. 'You've always avoided it.'

'I wish I'd avoided you,' she flung back at him, rushing from the room with a sense of panic.

She heard Dodie call after her, then the door slammed shut and she bolted for the theatre exit.

Katrine ran down to the willow-fringed river and walked fast beneath the green boughs, her eyes brilliant with anger. Yet somewhere at the back of her mind a little voice was repeating all that Max had said, repeating it again and again. Chocolate-box people ... was that a fair description of the Milfords? Then again she remembered Max's cool contempt as he said that she wasn't extended to her limit, and how he had called her a coward for running away from the theatre.

A coward? She stood still, staring into the slow-running waters. A flotilla of ducks steamed slowly towards her, hopeful of crumbs.

She stamped her foot, forgetting where she was in her rage. 'No, I'm not ...' she said aloud.

Behind her someone laughed and she turned quickly, going pinker. Nicky stood there, his golden head gleaming in the sunshine, his blue eyes full of charm.

'What was that about?'

She shook her head. 'Nothing!'

He gave her a wry glance. 'You've become very secretive, Katie.' He had called her that in their shared childhood, but she found she had an odd preference for the pet name Katya. She could not think why.

'Secretive?' she questioned.

'You didn't tell me you were coming to Cantwich,' he accused her with a reproachful look.

'You didn't tell me, either,' she said.

He laughed. 'Didn't I? Well, we haven't seen so much of each other lately.' He bent those blue eyes on her. 'We must remedy that.'

Her heart should have quickened. A year ago she would have been dumb with joy. Today she merely smiled, inwardly absorbed in what Max had said to her.

Nicky's brows drew together in affronted surprise. He was accustomed to seeing his plain little cousin light up whenever she set eyes on him. It was a novelty to have her almost indifferent to his company, and a novelty Nicky did not enjoy.

He took a closer look at her. She was really looking quite different, he realised. It was not merely the elegant clothes or the new hair-style. It was an inner glow which she had acquired. Nicky was puzzled. Was it possible that Katrine was changing? And if so—why?

Nicky walked back with her to the resumed rehearsal. They ran into a crowd of young actors and actresses who greeted them with warmth. Katrine was given a few sidelong, curious looks. She was still very much an unknown quantity to them.

Among them was the girl whose interest in Nicky she had noticed earlier, but today she was apparently deeply involved with another member of the cast, a sturdy dark-haired young man with a stubborn jaw. Nicky gave this pair a long, narrow-eyed look.

Katrine frowned. Nicky looked ... jealous? Irritated? Piqued? A mixture of all three, perhaps. Suddenly she thought, with a grimace, that this precisely described Nicky's attitude to herself lately. Was he only interested in a girl when he felt she might be losing interest in him? It was not a very admirable trait.

Max was waiting for them in the theatre bar. He gave Katrine a brief, cold glance as she came in with Nicky, but made no comment on her short absence. She, for her part, tried to be calm and efficient, but all the time her mind kept running over their earlier clashes, and she could not help asking herself: is he right about my voice?

She went to bed early that evening, pleading a headache, but lay awake thinking for hours.

Do I even want to consider such an upheaval in my life? she asked herself. Haven't I always wanted to be just an ordinary housewife? I love running a house, cooking, shopping and all the other domestic tasks. It gives me a sense of achievement...

That new little voice, at the back of her mind, asked cynically: do you? Do you, really? If you now have the chance to do something creative, exciting, something which will perhaps make Fra sit up and take notice... wouldn't you leap at the chance?

A shiver ran over her. Suppose one failed, after all...

She sat up. Cowardly! Max was right. She wanted to do something more than just exist, yet she was afraid of failure, and so she suppressed her secret dreams, turned away from them with a coward's dread.

She looked at the clock. Half past one! She suddenly felt hungry. She had had a tiny supper, eaten in bed—a light salad and black coffee. She had only had a few tiny sandwiches for lunch, too. No wonder she was suddenly ravenous.

She got out of bed and slid into her old dressing-gown, a faded lemon cotton which, together with the old lemon cotton pyjamas she was wearing, made her look like a little girl.

Tiptoeing downstairs, she paused to listen. Nothing stirred. Only the ticking of a clock, the hum of the refrigerator and the squeak of an open door at the end of the passage, swinging slightly in the summer wind, disturbed the silence.

She opened the kitchen door and went in, then stood, frozen, in the doorway as Max turned round and stared at her.

'Well, come in,' he said coolly. 'Don't just gape.

Hungry? So was I, so I've made myself an omelette. You can have half.'

'No, I'll get some cheese,' she refused.

'Indigestible stuff at night. Better have this,' he commanded with his usual decision, cutting a large, fluffy golden omelette in half and sliding the two halves on to two plates.

She hesitated, then accepted the fait accompli with a grudging sigh.

Max looked at her, his mouth twitching in amusement. 'Oh, your expression! Rebellious little creature, aren't you?'

'I'm sorry if that annoys you,' she retorted.

'Oh, it doesn't,' he said blandly. 'I find it stimulating. A little provocation works wonders.'

Katrine blushed, wondering what he meant exactly, yet not daring to ask. Her first forkful of golden egg brought a look of surprise to her face. He had beaten onion, ham and chives into the mixture. 'This is very good,' she told him, wonderingly.

He laughed. 'Don't sound so astounded. Why shouldn't I be able to cook? I live alone. Eating out is not only dull but expensive.'

She stared at him. She had never imagined his life at home, but now it occurred to her that he must live somewhere, eat, have his shirts laundered, have his bed made. Max was always so immaculately turned out, so elegant and supremely sure of himself, that she had almost believed he kept a flock of servants to support him. 'You do your own cooking?' she asked him in surprise.

'Most of the time,' he shrugged. 'My flat is serviced by a married couple, who are retained by the company who run the block of flats to do the cleaning, and they come to me for an hour each morning to do the usual housework. My cooking I do unless I bring back take-away food, as I often do, or some kind soul cooks for me.' His heavy-lidded eyes shot her a mocking look.

'A girl-friend?' she suggested, tongue in cheek.

'Precisely,' he agreed blandly.

'Not Dodie,' said Katrine thoughtfully. She could not conceive of Dodie acting as cook for Max. Dodie was waited on—she did not do the waiting.

'Dodie?' Max lifted his brows. 'Would you describe her as my girl-friend?' He watched Katrine intently as she flushed.

'Well, I ... that is ...' Her jumbled words died on her lips, and Max looked increasingly interested.

'I see that that's how you would have described her,' he murmured. 'How curious. Tell me, what else have you planned for us? A wedding, perhaps?'

'Don't tease!' she snapped, getting very red.

'Is this gossip fairly general?' he asked. 'Or was this idea your own discovery?'

She finished her omelette without answering. Max poured her a cup of cocoa from a large blue and white earthenware jug. 'This will help you sleep,' he said.

She was grateful to him for abandoning the subject. 'What a lot of cocoa,' she said lightly.

'I'm addicted to it,' he said.

Katrine drank hers rather quickly and stood up. Max raised a quizzical eyebrow. 'Going so soon? I shall have to finish this cocoa by myself. Is that kind?'

'I'm sleepy now,' she said lamely, wishing she could be as blandly unshakeable as Max always was. Had he any emotions at all behind that calm mask?

He opened the door for her, but as she slid past, nervously aware of him in his blue slacks and thin white shirt, he caught hold of her shoulder, his thumb rubbing gently along her shoulderbone beneath the cotton nightclothes. 'Katya,' he murmured softly, 'don't fight me. It only makes me more determined. Give in now and save us all time.'

She was not entirely certain what he meant, yet all her instincts rose inside her, fighting desperately against the spell Max could weave around a woman when he chose to exert that mocking charm of his. She did not trust him. She did not even like him. What was he trying to do to her, what were his motives?

She raised her blue eyes, their dark lashes flickering hard in an effort to push back unwanted tears of weariness. 'Why do you want me to have ambitions? We aren't all made of the same stuff. Some people ...'

'Some are born great, some achieve greatness and some have greatness thrust upon them,' he quoted drily. 'We all know Shakespeare's views on that. I'm in the business of creating stars ...'

She cut into his words with an expression of horrified disbelief. 'Stars! Stars? You must be mad! I'm not star material. I'm ordinary. Can't you see it?' She gestured down at her schoolgirlish cotton nightclothes.

Max laughed. 'Ordinary? You're as ordinary as dynamite!' He caught her by the shoulders, his fingers biting into her flesh, so that she raised her head, gasping.

'Max! You're hurt ...' The words were smothered beneath his lips as he bent his head and kissed her with violent intensity, so hard that it forced her head back and stretched her throat until it was painful.

She involuntarily closed her eyes, clinging to him without even knowing that she did so, while the whole world spun dizzily around her. A sensation of intolerable bliss burst upon her. She had never suspected that such emotions could exist.

Then she was free, her mouth stinging, her throat painful, her life torn up around her feet.

She looked at Max, swallowing hard. He thrust his hands into his pockets and rocked carelessly on his heels.

'It's time you grew up,' he said coolly.

She stared at him. Apart from the angry red which had invaded his face, he appeared to be totally calm, unmoved by what to herself had been a cataclysmic event. That kiss, which had thrown her from tranquillity into a state of tortured sensitivity, had apparently meant nothing much to Max. He had been teaching her a lesson by kissing her.

Through the drumming in her ears, the pounding of her pulses, she heard him speaking. 'I want you to think very hard about what Dodie and I have said to you. You've been shut away in your father's house all your life, hiding from any possibility of a challenge from life. But we all have to face the truth about ourselves. You're by no means ordinary, Katya —you've constantly underestimated yourself. Your family have helped. They formed your opinion of yourself, they quite unknowingly gave you a low idea of your own capabilities. The truth is that you only lack one ingredient of stardom...'

'Good looks,' she said huskily, striving for calm.

He shook his head, his eyes irritated. 'No. Confidence! Looks mean very little. But belief in oneself means everything.' He looked at her. 'Do you understand? Dodie and I want you to begin to have faith in yourself.'

'Dodie,' she murmured.

'Dodie believes in you, Katya.'

'Yes,' she said, nodding, her face softening. 'I love Dodie, too. But is Dodie's affection perhaps blinding her, deceiving her?'

'Don't be absurd,' Max said sharply. 'Dodie is a professional. No love could blind or deceive her. She's completely clear-headed where her job is concerned.'

Almost desperately she cried, 'I can't act! I have no stage presence. I'm clumsy, ugly and dull!'

Max moved angrily. 'Nonsense. That's for me to say.'

'You?' She frowned, looking bewildered.

'I might as well tell you now,' he said in a flat tone, 'I've decided to cast you as the Button Man's daughter.'

Katrine stood with her hands pressed against her sides, her face going painfully white, her great dark blue eyes enormous against the pallor of her skin. 'You can't be serious ... me? Act with Fra? Act professionally?' Her voice was hoarse, so choked that he barely heard what she said.

'You know the part,' Max said coolly. 'I've got an understudy reading it at present—the girl with freckles, cheerful little thing. She knows she's only understudy. I said I would announce the name of the actual actress later this week.'

She remembered very well. Everyone had wondered who would be joining them to play the part. She stared at him, aghast. He was talking perfectly calmly and seriously. He meant this!

'No, no,' she half sobbed. 'You must be mad ...'

He went on quite coolly, as if she had not said a word. 'It's only half a dozen lines, remember. For the rest of the play she's mute, shocked into withdrawal by the shooting of her brother years earlier. Only in the last scene does she speak, after her father dies, and then she makes a pathetic speech about life and death.'

'The part is impossible,' she said, searching for any avenue of escape. 'Even a good actress would find it hard.'

'True,' he nodded. 'Mime is never easy, but you

can do it. Cleo couldn't, not in a thousand years. But you could.'

His eyes held hers. She felt a strange sensation, a tingle of electricity, as if he was charging her mental batteries from his own high voltage personality. She realised he was willing her to accept, to believe in him and in herself. She could not tear her eyes away from the tranced spell in which his eyes held her.

'You can do this part, Katya,' he said softly, 'with me to help you.'

She was trembling, hypnotised by his curious, heavy-lidded eyes. Lamely, she said, 'Equity rules would forbid it. I'm not a member.'

He smiled, brushing this aside. 'We'll fix that. You're going to be a professional, you'll join Equity.'

'I can't do it!' she wailed in sheer desperation.

Max smiled. 'Yes,' he said very softly again.

She felt her limbs weaken, her power to resist him snapped. Max was watching her closely. He nodded, well content. 'You'll do it,' he told her. 'You'll do it for me.'

CHAPTER SIX

MAX made the announcement two days later. It came as a considerable shock to the other Milfords. Rolf looked aghast, as if he could not believe his ears, and he turned to Katrine, an anxious frown creasing his forehead, silently inquiring of her how she felt about the idea. She had been watching him, and when their eyes met she smiled quietly, forcing herself to offer a comfort she did not honestly feel able to give. The last thing she wanted was for Fra to suspect how terrified she was now.

Cleo had a dumbfounded expression for a second, then she turned and gave her sister a long, hard stare. Aloud, she asked, 'Katrine? Did you say Katrine?' Her tone was incredulous, exaggeratedly so.

Max calmly nodded. Dodie clapped her hands and smiled. 'It will complete the magic circle—all the Milfords will be in the business!' She spoke with childish gaiety. Anyone who knew her as well as Katrine would have known that Dodie Alexander was putting on a performance, acting for all she was worth, carefully pitching her response in order to smooth over the awkward first moments.

It was only later that Katrine realised the oddness of Nicky's reaction. He had been very quiet during the congratulations. Later, a smile pinned on his handsome face, he sauntered up and kissed her. 'Clever girl,' he murmured. And he winked.

She might not have thought anything of this, had he not been rather too obviously being discreet. His confidential aside had been pitched just high enough for Max to hear, while making it look as if it was a furtive whisper between the two of them.

She had flushed, catching Max's shrewd eyes on them. And Nicky had laughed again before sauntering away.

At that moment, Katrine had merely been unhappy at Nicky's assumption that she had planned all this. Later she saw that Nicky actually believed she was trying to ingratiate herself with Max in order to squeeze into the theatrical profession.

Max had got the point, too. He had said, in his office later, 'Your cousin is a poisonous little worm.'

'I'm sorry you heard what he said,' she apologised. 'I think it was a joke.' Hurriedly adding, 'In rather poor taste, I agree.'

'Poor? Disgusting, I would call it,' Max snapped. He had leaned back in his chair, surveying her. 'What the hell did you ever see in him?'

Her colour deepened. 'Nicky is a dear.'

Max's eyebrows rose steeply. 'A what? My dear girl, your blithe assumption that your fellow humans are all angels is enough to make strong men weep! Nicky is a typical Milford—selfish, vain and mindless.'

'Thanks very much,' she said tightly. 'Nice to know what you think of us.'

'I said a typical Milford. You're not a typical Milford. You're not typical of anything, in fact. You're one-off, unique.'

She felt her pulses leap and had to look away for fear of betraying herself. Sometimes she wondered if she had only imagined that Max kissed her in the kitchen, then she would remember vividly the weakening sense of bliss which had swept over her, and her body would come to passionate life. Until that moment she had barely known she had a body, had physical emotions as strong as this—now she knew herself better, and it terrified her.

She attended rehearsals now as a member of the cast, but as her one speech was so short she had very little to do at this stage. They had not yet advanced to the point where they combined movement and words. They were still feeling their way into the play.

Max was an intelligent director, letting the cast find their own way to an interpretation of the text. They discussed the play endlessly, both in and out of rehearsals. Often they sat in the theatre bar, sipping beer and talking long after Max dismissed them. Talk ranged from new clothes to poetry, from the price of fresh fruit to the latest cricket scores, but their favourite, their abiding topic, was of course the play. 'No shop talk,' some would cry now and then, but always the talk drifted back to what really consumed them.

Dodie was now giving Katrine private lessons in mime and stagecraft—how to walk, to stand, to turn. Katrine found, to her confounded astonishment, that she already knew these things as if by instinct. Dodie, triumphant, laughed. 'My darling Katya, you took them in with your mother's milk.' Then she looked thoughtful. 'Although, of course, you were actually bottle-fed.'

Katrine laughed. 'What a memory! Was I?'

'Yes, I remember very well. I had just started in the theatre and I saw you in your mother's arms. I was a child myself, full of the thrill of being in the theatre. It was a magic time for me. You were part of the magic, Katya darling.'

Katrine hugged her. 'You've been magic for me, too, dearest Dodie. Like another sister, or a very young mother...'

Dodie looked touched, moved, her sallow skin filled with warm colour.

Sebby trotted in with cold milk for them. 'Drink it up, Madame, while it's chilled. You don't like it when it gets warm.'

Dodie gave him a rueful glance. 'Bully!'

'Aren't all men?' said Katrine, thinking of Max.

Dodie laughed. 'How right you are, Katya!'

Katrine asked Dodie to help her with her part, to talk it over with her in detail. To her hurt surprise Dodie refused, gently but firmly.

'No, dear, that is Max's prerogative.'

'Oh, Max will dictate to me,' Katrine sighed.

'Max? He is far too clever a director for that,' said Dodie. 'You must feel the part yourself. Only you can project it. It must come from within yourself and nobody else...'

'I'm terrified of failing him,' Katrine admitted with a deep, sighing groan.

Dodie looked at her lovingly. 'You have humility, my dear—such a wonderful virtue.'

'If it's not taken to extremes,' Max drawled behind them, and Katrine felt her pulses leap. She did not turn to look at him. Her cheeks were too flushed, her eyes too bright.

Dodie left them quietly. Max perched himself on

the edge of a table, staring at Katrine's bent head.

'Time we had a chat, you and I.'

'Is it?' she asked huskily.

'I've been waiting for you to come to me.'

She slid him a sideways look, shy and uncertain. 'Oh? What about?'

'This part. You're in something of a special position—a newcomer to the profession, an amateur in many senses, who's never learnt the techniques we all use. I knew Dodie would help you with the physical side of it ...'

'She has,' she broke in eagerly. 'She's been marvellous—I feel much more at home on a stage now.'

He nodded. 'Good. Good. But that's only the beginning. Now you have to think about this girl you're playing—what makes her tick, what sort of girl she is ... You have to show the audience what sort of girl she is, remember, and you have no words to do that with—the author didn't see fit to give you any words. You have to do it all yourself.'

Panic thrust upwards into her head. She looked up at him, pale now, sweating. 'Max ... I can't! I don't know how ...'

'Because you've never thought about her, about what it feels like to be a girl in her position. At the moment all you're thinking about is yourself, how you're going to feel standing out there in front of an audience. But it won't be you, Katya.' He stood up and bent forward, his face inches from hers, his eyes compelling her to listen attentively. 'It will be another girl, a girl who's been shocked into a silent world by a tragedy she can't bear to face. Once you let yourself go, and sink your own personality inside that girl's mind, you'll begin to know what being an actress means.'

The words burst upon her like fireworks on a dark sky. She felt a sudden comprehension, a quick, clear knowledge flowering inside her. 'Max,' she breathed, 'I never thought of it like that. I see what you mean.'

She had always seen the theatre through the eyes of her family, and for the golden Milfords that meant charismatic performances in plays especially chosen as a fitting frame for their talents. She had rarely heard any of them talk as Max had just talked. All of them—Rolf, Cleo, Viola, Cass—were famous precisely because they always appeared as themselves, whatever the part. They did not act so much as dazzle. delight, enchant their audiences. She could not imagine Cleo sinking herself into the character of a tragic mute who is only seen in shabby rags! In this production, for instance, she wore a succession of gorgeous costumes and was apt to pose becomingly in a variety of positions around the stage.

Excited, strung up, Katrine felt for the first time a strange tingle of power, an electric shock of self-knowledge which she barely comprehended. I can do this part, she thought. That girl ... I understand her. Her world is too violent, too painful, to bear. She has to escape from it. She flies to safety, to silence. She ceases to be involved. She knows that involvement leads to more pain, so she withdraws altogether.

She moved around the room restlessly, thinking so fiercely, with such intensity, that she ceased to be aware of Max. He stood watching her, his hands in his pockets in a characteristic pose of lazy indifference, his head to one side and a faint, triumphant smile on his face.

Suddenly she came face to face with him. She was frowning, her face pale and absorbed.

Max did not speak. He just watched her, one eyebrow lifted in quizzical appraisal.

'Well?' He spoke at last, since Katrine had said nothing, merely staring at him out of huge blue eyes which he was well aware were not even seeing him.

She blinked and the new look of hungry absorption drained away, leaving her laughing shyly, in self-mockery. 'I'm sorry, I was miles away.'

'Worlds away, I would say,' he drawled. The heavy-lidded eyes were fixed on her, making her suddenly uncomfortably aware of him.

He was wearing a thin white shirt, open at the throat. His supercilious profile, his bony nose and strange eyes, had always had an odd effect upon her, but she knew now that for her Max was maddeningly attractive. She would have liked to deny it to herself, but honesty compelled admission.

Ever since he kissed her she had known the truth. Nicky's more obvious attractions had ceased to have any interest. She almost laughed aloud at the idea that anyone could prefer Nicky to Max. Nicky was immature, crudely obvious and had all the Milford faults—selfishness, vanity, lack of fidelity. When Max had told her that Nicky was all these things, she had angrily denied it. Now her own heart and mind had confirmed Max's opinion of her cousin. Nicky was charming but worthless.

She smiled at Max, unaware that for the first time in her life she was exuding confidence, charm, self-awareness. The glow which surrounds any woman in love was fully switched on for Katrine at that moment. She was as radiant as a summer sunrise.

Max drew a sharp breath, moving towards her. She looked up at him, her lips parted on a silent sigh.

Then an image of Dodie flashed into her mind, and she involuntarily stepped backwards, going pale.

She had forgotten Dodie for a few moments. Dodie Alexander, whom she had always loved as another sister, Dodie whose marriage had ended tragically and who deserved any reward and comfort life might offer her ...

Max halted, frowning, looking at her in sharp inquiry.

'I must ring Nicky,' Katrine blurted out crudely, seizing on her first excuse to hand. 'I promised to meet him tonight for a stroll before dark.'

She fled, and Max stared after her with a blank expression.

Nicky was staying locally, in a quiet pub on the

main London road, along with several other members of the cast. Katrine rang him, feeling that she wanted to talk to someone, and Nicky at once asked her round for a drink.

'I feel like walking,' she said. 'It's a lovely night.'

'Fine,' Nicky agreed. 'Meet you outside your place in fifteen minutes.'

His small sports car zipped towards her exactly on time, skewed to a dramatic halt and he leaned over and opened the door on her side.

'Hop in, sunshine.'

As she obeyed she heard the grate of a foot on the path. Max was standing outside the house, watching them. His face wore an inscrutable expression.

Nicky gave him a faintly mocking wave. Max made no gesture in response.

Nicky drove to a quiet country lane, parked in the entrance to a meadow and smiled at her. 'This do for your stroll?'

There was a sign indicating that a right of way ran through the meadow, so they climbed the stile set to the side of the gate and began to stroll quietly along the edge of the field. Some cows were occupying the far side of it, gently grazing on luscious long grass, thistles and buttercups. The footpath had obviously been carefully tended quite recently. The grass was short, the brambles and hawthorn hedge had been cut back so as not to impede passage and it was clear that many people utilised this short cut to the village in the valley below.

'Someone has done a good job on this footpath,' she said to Nicky.

'One of the rambling societies, probably,' he agreed. They talked lightly about rights of way, and Nicky laughed as she described a book she had once read about a fight between a ramblers' society and a local squire who wished to close a footpath which had been in use for centuries. In England these rights are taken very seriously. Once a footpath has been legally declared a public right of way, no one can close it with impunity, and local people often go to extraordinary lengths to fight landowners who try to stop them crossing their land by ancient paths.

They passed between an orchard on the left and a field of barley on the right and came down to a cutting in the hill through which ran a railway line. They crossed the narrow iron bridge, leaning over to stare down the straight silent track, running between high green banks.

'We ought to turn back,' Nicky said.

Katrine nodded reluctantly. The air was warm and sweet, the silence refreshing. She had enjoyed her walk. She looked at him with affection. Despite his many faults, he was, and would always be, one of her favourite people. 'Odd how growing up together has the effect of cancelling out other things,' she said vaguely.

Nicky laughed. 'What a very ambiguous remark! What's it supposed to mean?'

She laughed at herself with him. 'Oh, I don't know. That whatever the future brings, we still feel close to those we grow up with, I think.'

He looked down at her curiously. 'You've changed,' he half accused.

'Don't we all? Look at Cleo! What a change in her since we were children.'

'Oh, Cleo,' he said flatly.

'You and Cleo don't get on, do you? I should have thought you had a lot in common.' She looked at Nicky thoughtfully.

'Cleo expects every man she meets to kneel and burn incense at her shrine,' he said cuttingly. 'She can't stand me because I refuse to fall on my knees and worship.'

She nodded. 'Yes, I'd noticed that. She definitely resents your lack of interest.' Rather teasingly she added, 'But Cleo says the same of you, you know.'

He stared in affront. 'What do you mean? What does she say about me?'

'That you're only too well aware of your handsome face, and expect every girl to fall flat at the sight of it,' she said, tongue in cheek.

He went red, his blue eyes furious. 'Oh, does she? Kind of her! And is that what you think, too? That I'm vain and silly?'

'You're being silly now,' she said lightly. 'It's far too beautiful an evening to quarrel. Come on, I'll race you back to the car.'

Nicky abandoned his wounded vanity and loped after her up the footpath, flashing past her half way across the meadow, with the cows staring plaintively at them from the far side.

They stopped at his pub for a glass of lime and lager which they drank in the dusky garden under some shady sycamore trees. A blackbird chanted hypnotically from a song post behind them. Night-scented stocks filled the air with their perfume. Far away came the long-drawn-out wail of a train, rattling through the valley.

Nicky told her some funny stories about others in the cast, and then said suddenly, 'I underestimated you, sunshine.'

Katrine looked at him shyly. 'Did you?'

He winked. 'You bet I did! It never entered my head that anyone could take the great Max Neilson for a ride, but you did it, Katie, and I take my hat off to you. You have Max eating out of your hand. Everyone is staggered, you know. For him to cast you as the dumb girl is so amazing! Especially as you've never stepped on to a stage before! You may look a little innocent, but you've got hidden depths.'

She was pale now, wincing at what he had said. So that's what the rest of the cast thinks! she said to herself. They think I somehow influenced Max into giving me the part. They think I'm a scheming little cheat without any talent who's used Max to get what she wants.

It hurt. She looked at Nicky sadly. He was grinning, admiring and amused. His angle on life was so different to her own that they lived in different worlds. He thought that to cheat and scheme was admirable, if successful. He had no idea what she was like. No notion at all.

She was late getting to bed. She slipped through the kitchen and upstairs without meeting anyone. The house was dark and quiet. But as she came out of the bathroom ten minutes later, in her cotton pyjamas and dressing-gown, she bumped into Max.

He looked at her coolly. 'You must be in bed early now that you're working. No more late nights. Don't forget in future. I expect total obedience from my cast. You'll need all your energy and all your strength for the job.'

Katrine ducked her head, nodding silently.

He stood for a second or two, as if expecting her to argue or anyway reply, then he stood aside and she darted past and back to her own room.

Next morning he told her curtly that he was going to give her special rehearsals of her own at first. 'I'll take you through your part back here for a couple of days, then we'll rehearse on stage. You'll find it harder to remember movements than the others do as you're so inexperienced. When I think you're ready, you can join rehearsals with the rest of the cast again. Stay at home today and read the play on your own, taking a close note of your part.'

'Couldn't I do that at general rehearsal? Why must I do it alone?'

'Because I want you to feel more confident before I plunge you into public rehearsal. The others are going to be watching you with close interest, and that will make you nervous. You need all the confidence you can get as it is—I won't add to your burden by exposing you to the criticism of the others yet.'

That evening, after supper, Max marched her off to a quiet little room at the back of the house which they used as a spare reception room when any visitors clashed. If Rolf brought some friends home at the same time as Cleo arrived with a party of the cast, Rolf would take his friends into the spare sitting-room. Naturally, the local Festival Committee had been very hospitable towards these famous visitors. They had had to fend off many invitations, but Rolf enjoyed evenings spent accepting hero-worship, so he had seen a great deal of local people, and he had had to return their hospitality from time to time.

Max pushed the chairs back from the centre of the room, leaving it clear.

'Now,' he said, 'let's take a look at what you have to do ...'

They read through the part carefully, noting movement and gesture. Most of the time she was on stage, Katrine would be very still. The girl was a withdrawn character. She rarely moved, never spoke.

'But she is there,' Max emphasised. 'The audience can see her. So what is she doing?'

'Just sitting there?' suggested Katrine tentatively.

'Her father is talking about sending her to a hospital,' Max said quietly. 'Do you really think she doesn't react? She doesn't say anything. Flint doesn't even tell us what she does. But she's listening—so she must react. You have to show the audience that she understands what's going on...'

They moved on to the next scene, where Max again revealed to her his own sure grasp of the interaction of these characters, while showing her, too, how little she yet knew of the play. She had thought she knew it by heart, yet she had only had a very hazy idea of what would be happening on stage.

When they halted, she smiled at Max. 'You've been wonderful. I really feel I'm beginning to feel my way through the scenes.'

'You've barely scratched the surface,' he said curtly.

His tone made her stiffen. 'Well, we've made a start, anyway. Thank you.'

'For doing my job?' His tone was sarcastic.

She looked at him doubtfully. 'Max...'

'Yes?' He stood at the door, his hand on the door handle, looking at her unsmilingly.

'Is anything wrong?'

'Should it be?' He still spoke coolly.

She swallowed. 'You sound... very disagreeable.'

'Do I?' He did not unbend. His whole attitude made it clear that he was only waiting for her to release him from this pointless conversation. She made a gesture of finality and he at once opened the door and walked off without saying anything further.

Katrine saw nothing of him for the rest of the evening. He and Cleo vanished, presumably off to yet another local party. Cleo was in constant demand with the young men of the area, but she rationed her public appearances carefully. She had no intention of losing her glamorous image by being too accessible.

As rehearsals proceeded, Katrine grew more and more confident. Max was gently encouraging, praising her when things went well and comforting her when she lost her grip on the character. She found herself thinking about this girl all the time. At night her head was full of a tangled jumble of ideas. She often dreamt that she really was the girl. Her sense of pain in these dreams was so deep, so intense, that she once or twice woke sweating, in tears.

'I think you're ready to join the rest of the cast again,' Max told her at last.

There had been much speculation, she had gathered, as to why Max was keeping her apart. Not even her father or Cleo had ever been present when Max worked with her. Cleo was openly curious about their working methods. She teased and mocked Katrine on the subject whenever she got the chance.

'I can imagine what you get up to with Max! It's the perfect excuse for a quiet flirtation!'

Aware of Dodie at the breakfast table, listening, Katrine was vehement. 'Don't be absurd!'

'Then why are you so pink?' Cleo laughed cattily.

'I am not pink!'

'You're the colour of a beetroot, isn't she, Dodie?' Cleo's smile held malice as she glanced at Dodie. Lately, Katrine had noticed, Cleo was showing an increasing dislike of Dodie, a spite she had only recently begun to manifest. Had Dodie noticed? And did it hurt her? Katrine was concerned and puzzled.

Dodie looked at Cleo calmly, her brows faintly raised. 'You should not tease Katya.'

'No, of course, she's perfect, isn't she?' Cleo snapped, leaping to her feet. She slammed out of the room, leaving Katrine dazed and taken aback.

'What's the matter with her?' she asked Dodie unhappily. 'Lately she's been absolutely foul.'

'She is unhappy, poor Cleo,' Dodie murmured.

'But why?' Katrine was dumbfounded. Why was Cleo unhappy? Cleo, the most beautiful of all the Milfords, with her horde of fans and her reputation as the sex symbol of the age! What could possibly be making her unhappy?

The Mayor of Cantwich was throwing a large party for the company on the following evening. For the occasion a crowd of London journalists descended upon the little town.

'Probably drink the pubs dry in twenty-four hours,' Rolf grinned.

Katrine was reluctant to attend since Max had already warned her that the press were buzzing with interest in her.

'What did you expect? You're the Milford who escaped the net. Now you've been trapped. You'll be released into the public arena tomorrow night to be eaten by the wild beasts of Fleet Street.' Max was icily cynical, his supercilious features bored.

Dodie listened with a slight frown, her eyes puzzled. 'Max, you are terrifying the child! He is joking, my dearest! Max, tell her it will not be so bad.'

He shrugged. 'As you please, Dodie. I'm exaggerating.'

Dodie gave him an indignant glance. 'Katya, we shall be with you all the time. We will shield you from them, don't be alarmed. There is nothing to worry about.'

Later, she asked her, 'What is wrong between you and Max, my love?'

Katrine laughed lightly. 'Wrong? Nothing, Dodie. I think he's rather tired of coaching me, that's all.' She was becoming a conscious actress at last, she told herself bitterly as she climbed into bed that night. Once upon a time she could not have lied to Dodie so convincingly. Now it was becoming second nature to act a part.

She was leaving rehearsals on the next evening when she bumped into a familiar figure lurking on the river bank outside the theatre. She was not surprised when he hailed her.

'Hi there, Cinderella!'

'Roddy Sumner! I wondered if you would be coming down,' she said, not entirely displeased to see him. He had, after all, always been the only pressman to recognise her in the past. He had been kind and pleasant to her when she was of no use to him in his job. She knew only too well the sort of journalist who is as sweet as honey when it pays him only to turn nasty once someone ceased to be useful. It was almost as if some men hate successful people, and only live for the moment when they can with impunity insult and humiliate those whom they have had to be polite to in their days of triumph.

He looked down at her with interest. 'You've certainly changed since I last saw you.'

She was wearing her cinnamon trouser suit, her hair was brushed and shining in its elegant little bell around her face. She smiled. 'For the better, I hope?'

'Fishing, Cinderella?' He grinned mockingly. 'As if you need to be told! You look like a different girl. I always told you that you had something special, didn't I?'

'You said I was interesting because I was unlike the rest of my family,' she reminded him.

'And you misunderstood me,' he nodded. 'I was trying to tell you that not every man wants to marry a sex symbol. Most men prefer girls like you, with warm, sensitive faces and a genuine smile. You can be quite something when you smile, you know, Cinderella.'

'Why do you keep calling me that?' she asked half in irritation, half in amusement.

'It suits you,' he said. 'And I bet half Fleet Street will use it tomorrow. Your story is going to be big news. Quite a romance, suddenly being picked for a leading role when you're an unknown.'

'I only have one speech,' she said flatly. 'And I do come from a theatrical family. All my family are in the business.'

'Especially Miss Sex Symbol herself,' Roddy murmured, with a grimace as Cleo strolled towards them.

She paused, eyeing him icily, and he gave her a deep, mocking bow. 'Don't let us keep you from more important matters, Princess.'

Cleo flashed him a hard look. 'I won't! Katrine, are you coming? If you hang around here a big bad wolf may come along and eat you up.'

'Grrr!' growled Roddy, showing his white teeth.

Cleo tossed her head irritably, but otherwise ignored him. She looked at Katrine with a compelling glare. 'Come on...'

'May I be your escort to the big party tonight, Cinderella?' Roddy asked winningly. 'I promise not to eat you up despite what Grandmother just said.'

'We'll all be going together,' Cleo said quickly.

'Oh? Making the big entrance, eh?' Roddy looked cynically at her. 'And who'll be hogging the limelight, I wonder? It won't be little Cinderella, not if I know the Magnificent Milfords! She has as much chance of competing with you as she has of going six rounds with Butcher Brown, the Balham all-in wrestler.'

Cleo's face wore a frozen look of hostility as she glared at him. 'And of course your invitation has no connection with any desire to cut out your rivals and get an exclusive from our little innocent abroad?'

Roddy laughed insolently. 'Cinderella's a big girl now. Let her judge for herself what my motives are.'

Katrine looked at him in some puzzlement. She did not know his motives, but she did remember how often he had talked to her at similar parties in the past when everyone else had ignored her. Roddy had always made a point of finding her and making her laugh and feel more at ease. She smiled at him now. 'I don't see why I shouldn't go with you to the Mayor's party! My father is the star guest, not me.'

Cleo was furious. 'Wait until Max hears about this! He'll go berserk.'

'Let him,' Katrine said obstinately. Why should she go in fear of Max Neilson's reaction to anything? He had been perfectly beastly to her for days.

When she got back to the house she went into the kitchen to talk to Sebby, who liked to be kept in the picture about how rehearsals were going. She was eagerly telling him the latest development, when the door was suddenly slammed open, banging against the wall.

She turned, tense as a coiled spring. Max stood there, tight of lip and bleak of eye. 'Is Cleo telling the truth? Have you promised to go to this party tonight with Roddy Sumner?'

She saw from his icily controlled features that Cleo had not been speaking wildly when she said that Max would go berserk at the news. Max might be speaking carefully, coldly, but beneath those frozen words she glimpsed a rage she had never seen in him before, and her stomach turned over with dismay.

CHAPTER SEVEN

SHE pulled herself together, lifting her chin defiantly. 'Why shouldn't I go to the party with Roddy?'

Sebby discreetly slid out of the room, leaving Max facing her in grim silence.

'Have you forgotten that Sumner is a gossip columnist? Why do you imagine he has suddenly begun to take such an interest in you, you little idiot?'

'Roddy has always been a friend of mine,' she retorted. 'He was the only journalist I ever really knew well.'

Max laughed harshly. 'Clever Sumner, he cast his bread upon the waters and it came floating home tenfold, didn't it?'

'Don't be so cynical!'

His bleak eyes flashed at her. 'You don't imagine he was ever interested in you as a person, do you? You were one of the Milfords. You could drop useful titbits of information now and then. The Roddy Sumners of this world get a lot of their gossip from servants, relatives, hangers-on ...'

'Which category do I fit into?' she asked in sudden bitterness. 'Or is it all three? I've worked as a servant even though I'm one of the family, and I suppose I'm a hanger-on, too!'

Max frowned. 'Don't talk like that!'

'You implied it first!'

'I did nothing of the kind! You know very well I didn't mean that...'

She laughed. 'Do I? Well, whatever you meant, most people used to treat me with chilling indifference when I was just the girl who did all the work around the house. At parties they ignored me. If they saw me in the streets they didn't recognise me. They only wanted to know my sisters, the famous ones. I soon realised the difference between real friends and lip-service ones. Sebby and Dodie are the genuine article. You can trust and believe in them. Neither success nor failure make any difference to them.'

'And Roddy Sumner? What category does he fit into, in your book, Katya?' Max spoke quietly.

'Roddy puzzles me a little,' she admitted. 'It's true that he always made a point of searching me out and being friendly—true, too, that he never to my knowledge used me to find out something about my family. But I was never quite sure why Roddy was so nice to me. I used to wonder about it a lot.'

'Your instinctive common sense told you that he's one of the world's jackals,' Max snapped. 'He feeds on the fame of others. If he was nice to you there was an ulterior motive somewhere.'

She shrugged. 'Perhaps. I'm not sure. But I'll

never be sure if I avoid him. He asked me to go to the party with him, so I said I would.'

'You want to go, then?' Max surveyed her with narrowed eyes. 'How is sweet cousin Nicky going to like that?'

Katrine blushed. 'Nicky?' She had forgotten that she had given Max the deliberate impression that she was still in love with Nicky.

Max's mouth compressed. 'Don't tell me you've forgotten him already? Is there no faith in women, even the best of them?' His voice was harsh and raw with rage. 'I could have sworn that you ...' He broke off, gesturing savagely.

'Nicky didn't ask me to go to the party with him,' she pointed out, her face pale now at the cruelty of what he had just said to her. 'In fact, Nicky ... we ... he takes out other girls, you know. There's no engagement or even any specific understanding between Nicky and myself.'

'So what's sauce for the goose is sauce for the gander?' he said cynically. 'You're paying him back in his own coin? Showing Nicky that if he can take out other girls you can go out with other men?' He looked at her with cold dislike. 'How very feminine! You soon learn the old tricks, don't you?'

'Oh, you're so unfair,' she cried angrily. 'You keep putting words into my mouth, jumping to unjust conclusions! Why do you always put the worst construction on what I say and do?'

Max drew back his lower lip, his teeth showing in a faint grimace of self-mockery. 'Why, indeed?

It's none of my business what you do with your life. If you want to waste yourself on either of these worthless idiots, go ahead—I just thought you had more intelligence than that. Obviously I was wrong. You're another eternal female eager to seize what glitters prettily, even if it may turn out to be brass, not gold. Roddy Sumner and Nicky are two of a kind, hadn't you noticed?'

She looked at him, struck suddenly by the truth of what he said. Yes, Roddy and Nicky had much in common. They were both of them handsome, charming, flirtatious and successful with women.

She forced a smile. 'Perhaps I find the type attractive!'

Max's eyes narrowed on her face. 'So it would seem! What does that convey about your taste?'

Katrine shrugged. 'We all have different ideas about life.'

Max opened his mouth, then closed it again with a snap of anger. 'Very well,' he said tightly after a silent pause. 'Apart from any other consideration, you shouldn't have made separate arrangements to go to the party because the Milfords ought to be making a combined entrance. Cleo is very put out.'

'Cleo was put out because Roddy asked me instead of her,' said Katrine flatly. 'Cleo always resents it when a man shows any interest in anyone but herself—you know that. She doesn't want Roddy, but she has this dog-in-the-manger attitude. She feels insulted because he asked someone else. He wounded her pride.'

'Your father feels much the same, though,' said Max. 'He wanted you all to make a grand entrance.'

'I'm sorry,' Katrine said flatly.

'You want to steal their thunder, is that it? Sweep in alone and have all eyes riveted on you?' He smiled cuttingly. 'I didn't expect you to show these Milford traits. I thought you would be able to ride success, not let it ride you.'

She felt like stamping her foot, her anger burning inside her so that her cheeks were poppy red and her eyes flashed as she retorted, 'I don't have to stand here and listen to you insulting me! I haven't done anything so very dreadful—just accepted a simple invitation. Success isn't riding me, I can assure you. Good heavens, we haven't even reached the first night yet. I may be the biggest flop of all time— I probably will be. And at this precise moment I really couldn't care less. I wish I'd never said I would do this silly play. It seems to have given you the notion that you can say what you like to me and get away with it. Well, you're wrong! I won't put up with your arrogant, sarcastic, bullying tactics a moment longer. I'll stand down. You can put the understudy on—she'll only have one speech to learn. There's no risk involved. And I hope that will make you happy!' Then she turned and dashed from the room, slamming the door after her.

She ran upstairs, sobbing softly under her breath, her fists clenched into two tight balls at her sides.

Dodie, in a devastating gown of black lace, one crimson splash of silk at the deepest curve of her neckline to give colour to her face, came out of her bedroom and said vaguely, 'Do me up at the back, angel, will you?'

Katrine dared not even pause for fear of letting the brimming tears spill down her face, betraying her. 'Sorry,' she managed to whisper hoarsely, running past Dodie into her room.

She pushed home the bolt and leaned against the door for a second, heaving a sigh. Then the flood burst and she threw herself upon the bed, burying her face in her pillow.

Some time later, when her tears had subsided a little and she had wept herself into a form of calm, she heard a gentle tapping at the door. 'Katya dearest, let me in ...'

'I'm all right, Dodie,' she said huskily. 'Please, don't worry about me ...'

'I *am* worried,' said Dodie. 'Please let me come in and talk to you.'

Katrine sat up, wiping her face clumsily with the back of her hand in a childish gesture. She took several deep breaths, then stood up and went to the door.

Dodie was looking lovingly anxious when she came in, her dark eyes at once flying to Katrine's face. 'Oh, your poor little face!' she breathed. 'Sit down, child, and let me attend to it.'

Katrine obeyed her without further argument. Dodie produced a large bottle of cologne and some cotton wool balls. She gently, delicately, wiped Katrine's face and forehead with the sweet-scented cologne, cooling and refreshing her. 'What a display of temperament,' she murmured teasingly. 'I did not think you had it in you! You have made your eyes red and your lids are swollen. You must rest for an hour before the party with some pads on these poor eyes.'

'I'm not going to the party,' said Katrine.

'Of course you are,' Dodie insisted.

'You don't understand——' Katrine began.

'I have spoken to Max,' said Dodie. 'I know all about it. Max was very naughty to upset you, but Max has a temperament, too, you know, love. He may hide it under that cool manner, but Max is as emotional as any creative artist.'

Katrine was so surprised by this new idea of Max as an emotional creative genius that she just stared, open-mouthed.

Dodie laughed. 'Do not stare so! Did you think he ran on petrol instead of his own nerves like the rest of us? You must learn to consider things from other points of view beside your own. Max has worked very hard for this production. He has worked very hard to train you, dearest. He has been selfless, tireless and a tower of strength to the company. If now and then he blows his cool, can you not find it in you to forgive him?'

'I suppose so,' Katrine said slowly. 'Oh, Dodie, I feel a perfect worm. I resigned from the play. Did he tell you?'

Dodie laughed, kissing her on the top of her head. 'He told me you had threatened him with resignation—he did not believe you could be so cruel as to mean it after all we have done! What a waste of effort! No, no, you cannot resign.'

'And tonight? The party?' Katrine looked up at her, leaning her head against Dodie's waist.

'You will go there with the rest of us,' Dodie said firmly. 'Your father would, indeed, be angry if you did not. Roddy Sumner can join our party—that is the best solution. We can all go together.'

Katrine sighed. 'Well, if *you* say so, Dodie.'

Dodie looked at her with an odd little grimace of tenderness. 'Poor Max!'

Katrine frowned, a little bewildered. What did Dodie mean by that ambiguous remark?

'And Katya,' Dodie added. 'Be nice to Max, eh?'

Katya was to wear her black-and-white striped evening dress. Dodie insisted on helping her, brushing her hair and doing her make-up for the evening. Her deft thin fingers moved lightly over Katrine's face, doing magic things with little pots and tubes, and even Katrine was taken aback by the change she saw in herself.

She felt very conspicuous in her dress. Although it was demurely simple from the front, it was so very naked at the back, and Katrine was shaking with nerves as she and Dodie went down to join the others.

Rolf turned and looked at them, distinguished as ever in his evening clothes. His still blond beard bristled with pride.

'My two lovely girls,' he said, coming forward to

kiss them both fondly. 'You look ravishing, both of you.'

Sebby stared from Dodie to Katrine, his melancholy eyes narrowed. 'Look like mother and daughter, don't they?' he murmured.

Rolf started visibly. 'So they do! How extraordinary! I never noticed it before. Dodie, it must be fate!'

Dodie laughed and went pink. 'Rolf, don't be absurd! Katrine is nothing like me.'

Cleo was standing near the window with Max, watching the scene with hostile eyes. 'Touching, isn't it?' she observed to Max.

Katrine looked slowly, reluctantly, at Max. He was watching her, his mouth sardonic. Her lids fluttered revealingly, her colour ebbed.

'Are we all ready, then?' Rolf demanded.

'We're waiting for Katya's young man,' Dodie said.

Rolf's eyes widened. 'Young man? Who's that?'

'Roddy Sumner,' said Cleo viciously with a snap of her white teeth.

'The gossip columnist? Good lord, Katrine, do you know what you're doing?'

She looked uneasily at him. 'I think so, Fra.'

Rolf flung back his broad shoulders, looking more than ever like a handsome middle-aged Viking, the late evening sunlight glinting on his golden head from the window. 'I hope you do. I know they say any publicity is good publicity, but I'm not so certain. Sumner isn't a bad fellow, as these gossip hounds go, but he can hardly help having an ulterior motive, can he?'

'I like him, Fra,' she said unhappily.

'Hmmm...' Rolf looked at Dodie, raising his brows in a silent query. Dodie smiled reassuringly at him, shaking her head, and Rolf shrugged. 'Well, I see I must let you learn from your own mistakes. You've made precious few of them to date, I'll admit.' He grinned at Cleo. 'Your sisters have been known to make a few howling mistakes in the past, so we'll wait and see, won't we, Cleo?'

Cleo was not amused. She slid her hand through Max's arm. 'We'll wait in the car,' she said with frozen dignity.

As they passed her, Cleo averted her gaze, but Max met Katrine's eyes directly, his own glance penetrating, watchful. She tried to convey with her look an apology, an appeal, but his eyes did not relent. Then he was gone and she shivered miserably.

A few moments later Roddy arrived, dramatically striking in his evening clothes, his dark good looks set off by the frilled white shirt and black jacket. He wore a dark red carnation in a buttonhole, which he pulled out and presented to Dodie with an admiring bow. To Katrine he gave a tiny posy of old-fashioned English flowers, bound Victorian fashion in a silver holder. She was entranced by them. 'Oh, how lovely! Sweet william, pinks, forget-me-nots... that was sweet of you, Roddy!'

Dodie surveyed them tolerantly. Rolf shook hands with Roddy, smiling. 'How are you? Fine? Good.

Hope you're going to enjoy this party. They're a great set of people down here, you know—wonderfully hospitable. Kindness itself.'

They joined Max and Cleo outside. Roddy was driving his own car, a sleek white sports model with a retractable hood and a panel full of gadgets. As they climbed in, Max drove past, his profile haughtily averted. Roddy stared after them.

'I can never make out whether Neilson is dating your sister or Dodie Alexander.'

Katrine didn't answer. He glanced at her, then laughed. 'What's the matter? Did I step over the invisible line? Sorry, I'll be careful not to ask loaded questions in future, I promise. This time, I can swear on my honour, the question was purely casual —I didn't intend to use it in the column.'

'But if I'd answered it you might have used it,' she said quietly. 'The temptation would have been very great.'

Roddy groaned. 'Too true, sweetheart. Sorry, is my being here tonight going to be embarrassing for you? I thought I sensed a certain, shall we say, "freeze" around when I drove up. Neilson looked at me the way people look at a maggot they've found in their lettuce. Your beautiful but stuck-up sister didn't apparently see me at all. I was the invisible man to her. Am I jumping to conclusions, or did they flip their lids when they discovered I was joining the party as your escort?'

Katrine looked at him with sudden amusement.

'I'm sure you don't need me to draw you a diagram, Roddy.'

He grinned back, cheerfully irreverent. 'The Magnificent Milfords didn't fancy a mere newshound muscling in on their big entrance?'

'That's not exactly how I would have phrased it,' she said softly. 'But you're a gossip columnist, and some people might suspect you had an ulterior motive in anything you did.'

He looked thoughtful. 'Yes, oh, yes, I see. And what do you think, Cinderella?'

Her big blue eyes were wide and frank as she looked back at him. 'You've always been pleasant to me, Roddy, but I'm not altogether naïve enough to think you meant anything much by it.'

Roddy's handsome face darkened with sudden anger. 'My God, you must think I'm a worm if you think me incapable of an honest-to-God reaction to a girl like you. What do you think I am? Bluebeard? I like you, Cinderella. Look, I'll be completely honest. Your family are news. It's my job to watch them. You've become news too, now, so I automatically take an interest in you, professionally and otherwise. But I have standards, however low they may seem to you. There are some things I would never do, and one of them is to use a personal and private relationship in order to get a story. If I want to know something, I'll ask you and you can say yes or no as to whether you answer. I promise, Cinderella, I'll never make capital out of you.'

She looked at his serious, intent face and she believed him. 'All right, Roddy,' she said. 'It's a deal.'

He looked relieved. 'Great. Now, let's drop the subject. Nice to know what people think of you. I gather your sister regards me as lower than the dust beneath her chariot wheels.'

'She isn't struck,' admitted Katrine gently.

Roddy laughed. 'It's mutual!' He drove down the winding lanes with speed, zipping round corners at an angle which alarmed her. They had reached the Assembly Rooms, where the party was to be held, before she had time to breathe properly. She let out a long, nervous sigh of relief. 'I didn't think we'd make it! Do you always drive like that?'

'Is there another way?' Roddy parked the car as directed by a uniformed commissionaire, showed the ticket he had been issued with as a member of the press and was directed into the building.

A little crowd gathered outside buzzed with interest. 'Who's that? I don't know ... must be an actor and his girl-friend ... he's fantastic, just like a film star ... don't think much of her, though, do you?' The whispers reached them both and Roddy grinned.

Katrine laughed back at him. 'You do look like a film star, it's true. Did you ever think of going on the stage?'

'I had other fantasies,' he said. 'I dreamt of being the great crime reporter, tracking down criminals before Scotland Yard got to them. I got sidetracked into writing a gossip column years ago, and I've never fought my way out of it again.' He grimaced.

'Life does funny things to people. I never thought I would end up doing this job.'

'Is it too late to change?' Katrine asked.

He looked surprised. 'I don't know. I gave up my old dream a long time ago. I imagine it would be possible to move out of this way of life, but I doubt if I could switch to crime reporting now. You need years of apprenticeship to do that.'

'Isn't there anything else you want to do?' she asked.

Roddy shook his head. 'I always wanted to write a book, but that's another dream I abandoned.'

'You can always learn to dream again,' she said softly.

They paused in the foyer of the Assembly Rooms, waiting for the others to join them. Roddy looked down at her, his handsome face suddenly vividly excited. 'My God, Cinderella, you're quite a girl, do you know that? I love you passionately...'

He had spoken rather loudly in his excitement, and there was no doubt that both Cleo and Max, at that moment moving towards them, had heard. Katrine wore a half embarrassed, half touched smile as she glanced past Roddy and met Max's cold eyes. He was staring at her, narrowly, his expression hostile.

'What's this, true confession time?' asked Cleo in a spiteful drawl.

Roddy flushed slightly. He had not realised until then that he had been overheard.

With a relieved sigh, Katrine saw Rolf, Dodie and

a crowd of attendant journalists at the entrance. 'They're here!'

They all turned to watch as, kingly and smiling, Rolf led Dodie towards them, her hand clasped in his, her black lace skirts sweeping elegantly behind her.

'What a magnificent couple,' Roddy murmured. 'I remember them in *Hamlet* as Claudius and the Queen. They looked just like this!'

Katrine looked uneasily at Max. The thought had been occurring to her more and more often lately. Had it occurred to Max? Or was he emotionally blind to the absolute rightness of seeing Rolf and Dodie together like this?

'Ah, my dears, you're here,' Rolf observed with satisfaction. 'Then we're all ready. Come along!'

The doors were flung open. The Mayor and his lady were there, smiling, flushed, excited. The high-ceilinged room was filled to overflowing with local dignitaries and the rest of the company. Rolf and Dodie moved forward to a ripple of eager applause, with the others following in their wake like attendants upon a royal procession.

Katrine was almost unaware of the passage of time after that. She smiled, shook hands, made polite small talk. Faces swam before her eyes. Voices talked. She forced herself to keep smiling.

She lost Roddy somewhere, detained by a talkative local reporter, and found herself being buttonholed by a lady in mauve silk who wanted to discuss her teenage daughter's ambitions to go on the stage.

Katrine listened kindly, made the appropriate noises in response and felt increasingly weary. It was an effort to smile, to speak. So many strangers, so much noise. She was not used to being in the public eye. She had always been on the fringe, outside the eye of the storm. Suddenly she had been flung into the centre of the maelstrom, and she found it tiring beyond words.

'You look like death,' a voice said tersely as she turned away after yet another encounter with a total stranger. 'Come and have a drink.'

She did not need to look to know who it was, the tight syllables told her. His hand gripped her elbow in a vice. She had no option but to obey.

He pushed her into a corner of the huge room, down into a leather-seated chair out of sight behind a potted palm. For a moment he vanished, only to reappear with a drink in each hand. 'This will put some colour into your cheeks,' he said curtly.

She sipped, shuddered. 'Ugh, I loathe gin!'

'Drink it and shut up,' he snapped.

Katrine raised her weary lids to regard him unsmilingly. 'You big bully.'

His face was shadowed, unreadable. 'That dress is too sophisticated for you,' he said in sudden irrelevance.

'That was what I told Dodie, but she insisted.' Strange how the truth could sting, she thought with the aloof Olympian calmness which exhaustion can sometimes produce.

He studied her, eyes narrow. 'Yet in a way it suits

you—very demure at the first glance, covered-up and modest, only to startle later by being reckless and unexpected...'

She made herself look amused. 'Is that how you see me, Max?'

He leaned against the wall, staring down at her. 'Has anyone ever told you that you just beg for trouble?'

She felt her heart beating fiercely against her breast, a wild, suffocating excitement tingling along her veins. 'Do I?' Her weariness dropped away like a discarded cloak.

'You know damned well you do,' he muttered. 'Why did you come here tonight with Sumner if not to provoke some response from Nicky? Look at the way you've behaved with the two of them. If that isn't asking for trouble, I don't know what is!'

'I told you why I came here with Roddy,' she said. 'He asked me.'

'That simple?' His lips twisted in a half sneer. 'One only has to ask?'

Something in his expression made her tremble and look away. After a moment she said quietly, 'You're a strange man, Max. I don't understand you.'

'You're dead right,' he snapped. 'You don't understand me.'

They were silent for a few moments, as if neither cared to continue further along that line. Katrine felt an ache of misery begin inside her. She urgently longed to go home, to be alone, away from all this noise, colour, light.

Aloud she said suddenly, 'I hate parties!'

Max gave a brusque laugh. 'Do you? Why?'

She shrugged. 'It's a strain pretending to enjoy oneself...'

'Pretending?' The word was mockingly sardonic. 'You don't try very hard to pretend when you're with me.'

'You have an irritating habit of seeing through pretences,' she said in sudden direct honesty.

Either he had bent towards her, or she had raised her head, but it seemed that he was very close suddenly, his face just above hers, his eyes holding her gaze. She longed helplessly to reach up and press her lips against that sardonic mouth, kiss his hard cheek and the tough line of his jaw. Her body was swamped with feelings she could not control. Unknowingly, she half closed her eyelids, her bitten lips full with the moist bloom of passion.

Then the discreet band burst into a clashing chord, the microphone buzzed and the Mayor announced proudly that the supper room was now open. 'After supper there will be dancing...'

Max was standing erect again. Katrine was very pink, ashamed of herself for having come so close to an embarrassing display of emotion.

Nicky slid through the crowd. His bright gaze touched both their faces, curious, alert, amused. 'Can I take you in to supper, Katie?' he asked cheerfully.

She hesitated, glancing at Max for a lead. With wry mouth and averted eyes he moved away.

'Thank you, Nicky,' she said very loudly, her shame making her angry.

'You and Max have a funny relationship,' Nicky said thoughtfully. 'He's always very protective towards you, but in an angry way. I suppose he's ashamed of feeling fatherly towards a girl of your age.'

'Fatherly?' The word somehow offended her.

'Protective,' Nicky expanded. 'Max is the type who hates to admit he has feelings. He's tough both on stage and off.'

'He was a good actor, wasn't he?' she said.

'He makes a better director,' said Nicky. 'I always thought Max rather too buttoned-up to make a good actor—at least, to make one of the best. He's far too introverted, intellectual. I hate clever actors. Give me someone like your father any day.'

She laughed. 'Better not let Fra hear you say that! He thinks he *is* a clever actor.'

Nicky grinned. 'He isn't. He's instinctive.'

'That's what Max said,' she murmured, struck by the coincidence.

'Is it?' Nicky looked flattered. 'Well, well, great minds think alike, it seems. Nice to know Max agrees with me.'

Katrine gave Nicky a shy, uncertain look. 'Nicky, you would tell me the truth, wouldn't you?'

He looked alarmed. 'That depends on the question.'

'How do you honestly think I'm doing with the play?' she asked him.

Nicky was relieved. 'Oh, is that all? You're good, Katie. You've got natural talent. You certainly surprised me.'

She looked hard at him, trying to read his mind. 'You mean that?'

'Why should I lie to you? Of course I mean it. You're never going to be a sex symbol like Cleo, but you may end up being a much better actress than either of your sisters.' Nicky was astoundingly casual about it, speaking lightly and without emphasis. His face was as transparent as well water. Katrine could not help but see that he meant every word.

She flushed deeply. 'Thanks.' Her gratitude made her smile at him with all her old affection, the now worn-out tenderness of her brief infatuation replaced by a new warmth towards her childhood companion and lifelong friend.

Nicky slid an arm around her waist and bent to kiss her lightly on the lips. 'Think nothing of it, sweetheart. We're all in the business now.' He winked. 'Consultations free, to the family.'

Cleo, walking into the supper-room with Max, paused to look sharply across the room at her younger sister and Nicky. Her lovely face wore a cruel half-smile as she watched Nicky kiss Katrine. 'How touching,' she observed to Max, who had also observed this. 'My little sister is knee-deep in admirers since she launched out into show business. Quite a transformation scene! The ugly duckling turned swan, pulling the men like a magnet! If Nicky doesn't watch out he'll find himself married, and the marriage state wouldn't suit dear Nicky.'

'I wonder,' Max murmured drily.

CHAPTER EIGHT

THE supper tables were impressively laid out with great baskets of flowers arranged at intervals along their length. Carnations, gladioli, roses gave colour, perfume and beauty to the room. Above their heads hung chandeliers glittering and tinkling in a faint breeze.

The Mayor made a brief speech of welcome to the company. Rolf then replied with a speech praising Pascal Flint and, by discreet implication, the citizens of the little town from which he had sprung. He made a few jokes at which everyone laughed, then several other people made speeches before, at last, the cold buffet was free to be consumed.

The food was superb. Canapés, salty with anchovies; caviar like tiny seed pearls gleaming black against the rolled bread and butter it was served with, thick slices of quiche lorraine, devilled eggs on lettuce and a dozen other rare delicacies.

Roddy loomed as Nicky brought Katrine a plateful of these delicious trifles. 'Pirate!' He glared at Nicky. 'You snatched my girl!'

'Once aboard the lugger, you know, old man,' mocked Nicky.

Roddy gave her a soulful look. 'Aren't you going to remember I brought you, Cinderella? Is it kind to desert me?'

She laughed. 'Why don't you join us?'

Nicky scowled. 'He doesn't need encouragement. You know what his fellow hacks call him? The Amoeba.'

She giggled. 'Oh, I don't believe that.'

Roddy growled. 'It's a dirty lie. That isn't what they call me at all.'

Nicky gave him a wide-eyed innocent smile. 'What do they call you, then?'

Roddy looked blankly at him. He didn't answer.

'Oh, yes,' said Nicky sweetly, 'I remember——'

'Shut up,' Roddy broke in angrily. He was rather red and seemed seriously put out. Nicky grinned, sipped his champagne without saying anything else. Katrine wondered what nickname his fellows gave him, and why it made him so angry. She looked at Nicky rather reproachfully, but he just winked and seemed rather pleased with himself.

She nibbled at her little hoard of food without appetite. She was being very careful not to look across the room at Cleo and Max, seated in a corner, close together, the dark head near to the gold one.

'Tell me, Milford,' Roddy said casually above her head, 'What exactly is the situation with Max Neilson? Is he dating Dodie Alexander or not? And if he is, why does he see so much of Cleo Milford?'

Nicky slowly chewed a piece of ripe Brie, swallowed it. Then he looked up at Roddy, his handsome face insolent. 'Why don't you ask Max himself?'

Roddy laughed shortly. 'And get my face pushed through the back of my head? No, thanks.'

Nicky looked him over contemptuously. 'Brave, aren't you?'

'That isn't an essential qualification for my job,' Roddy said coolly.

'No—sheer nerve comes top of the list, doesn't it? Run close by consummate cheek, thickness of skin and absence of principles.' Nicky sounded bitter. It surprised Katrine. She had never heard him speak so sharply to a member of the press. Usually he was very careful not to offend them.

Roddy grimaced. 'You're still brooding over that paragraph I ran on you and the delectable Delia,' he said lightly. 'Sorry if it trod on your toes, but I was only doing my job. It came to my ears that you and Delia were having a fling together, so I printed it. Could I have know you were just at the end of the affair and that publicity at that moment would be so embarrassing?'

Nicky smiled, showing all his teeth. 'No, you couldn't have known, just as I couldn't know that you didn't want anyone calling you Big Ears in front of your female friends.'

'Big Ears?' Katrine could not stop giggling.

'What else can one call a gossip columnist?' asked

Nicky very sweetly. 'Suits him, doesn't it?'

Katrine laughed. Roddy straightened, very red. He looked at Nicky with menace in his eyes.

'I ought to punch your head, Milford.'

'You can try,' Nicky smiled.

There was a little buzz of interest among the people nearby. They openly stared, hearing the anger in the men's voices. Katrine said urgently, 'Stop it, both of you! Do you want to ruin this party for everybody else?'

Then Max was there, very tall, very cool, very supercilious. His grey eyes were bleak as he surveyed the three of them. Katrine flinched from the contempt she saw in his face.

'Right,' he said softly, yet with an icy wind blowing in his voice. 'That's enough. I don't know what caused this little fracas, but I do know it stops right here and now. Smile, all of you, and keep smiling. Sumner, go and get yourself some food and keep away from Nicky for the rest of the evening. Nicky, go and take Cleo through to dance.'

Roddy moved off without a word. Nicky looked at Katrine quickly. 'Darling...'

'Yes, go and dance with Cleo,' she urged.

He nodded and went. She sat, her hands loosely holding her plate. Max removed it.

'Want any more?'

'No, thank you,' she said politely.

'Champagne?'

'No, thank you.'

'Then come and dance,' he said tersely.

She hesitated.

He leant down a thin, strong hand and yanked her to her feet with a remorseless movement. 'If you ever make me really angry,' he said at her ear, 'you'll be extremely sorry.'

She had never heard him speak so savagely, so bitingly before. She lowered her head and permitted him to steer her across the room towards the sweet sound of music.

They stood on the edge of the dance floor for a moment. A number of couples were already dancing. She saw Nicky and Cleo circling in silence. A spot of bright red burnt on each of Cleo's cheeks. Her eyes were brilliant, hard, angry, and she stared over Nicky's shoulder with a set expression.

Katrine dared not look at Max for fear of him reading her expression. The very thought of being in his arms, of dancing close to him, was making her tremble inwardly and her nerves were jumping.

Suddenly he swung her into his arms, his hand closing firmly on her waist. The band were playing a quickstep, but after a moment they changed to a dreamy waltz. Max's long legs were surprisingly agile, and she found it easy to follow his firm, deft lead.

'You see now what happens when you play off one man against another,' Max said sharply at her ear.

She glanced up warily. His face was set mercilessly.

'They didn't quarrel over me,' she protested.

'No?' His lip curled in a sneer.

'It was something about a story Roddy once wrote about Nicky and a girl called Delia,' she said.

Max shot her a narrowed glance. 'Delia Brett?'

'I don't know. They didn't say.' She waited a moment. 'She isn't an actress, is she?'

'No,' Max said. 'She's a singer, a very bad one, but pretty. She and Nicky went around together for a while before she married.'

'Who did she marry?'

'I forget. A dog biscuit king, I think. Someone with money. Delia almost didn't make it to her millions, though—Roddy Sumner printed a story about her and Nicky just at the wrong moment.'

'Oh, that was it?' She frowned. 'But it was all right in the end, wasn't it?'

'No thanks to Sumner,' Max said curtly.

'He couldn't have known!'

'Oh, he knew! Roddy Sumner hears everything.'

'That's why they call him Big Ears,' she said involuntarily, then giggled, clapping her hand to her mouth.

Max looked down at her, holding her a little away from his chest. His supercilious features were relaxed in amusement. 'So you heard that, did you? Suits him, doesn't it?' He grinned.

'But if you're right, it was very wrong of Roddy to print that story. It might have wrecked Delia's life.'

'Sumner feeds on disaster,' Max said. 'He's a leech, sucking the blood from his victims.'

Katrine was bewildered. She had liked Roddy so

much. He was so pleasant, so friendly. She had believed him to be sincere. Why had he printed that story about Delia? she wondered. She could not fit this image of him into the picture she had already formed from her own observation. It was possible that she had been misled, of course. He might be a very cunning, hypocritical man. But she still did not quite believe him to be as bad as Max claimed.

'I'll tell him you won't be requiring his services as escort home,' Max murmured.

'No,' she said quickly. She did not want to cut Roddy out of her life without finding out the truth for herself.

Max looked down at her, a glint of anger in his grey eyes. 'What do you mean, no? After what you've just heard about him, you still mean to go on seeing him?'

'I want to hear the truth from his own lips,' she said with a trace of stubborn independence that surprised herself.

'My dear girl,' Max drawled with all his old patronage, 'you surely don't expect to get the truth from a gossip hound? He'll tell you what suits him.'

Stung, she said, 'I think I can distinguish the truth from a lie.'

He laughed harshly. 'You're joking, of course!'

'No, I'm not,' she said crossly. 'Don't make fun of me, Max. I'm not a little girl.'

'Then why behave like one? You're talking like a naïve fool. Sumner has been pulling the wool over your innocent little eyes for months. At last someone has managed to make you see what a cheat he is, but you still insist on giving him the benefit of the doubt! Is that the action of a sensible person?'

'It's the action of a friend,' Katrine said obstinately.

'A friend?' His eyes raked her furiously. 'Are you sure that that's all you are?'

'Yes,' she said huskily, flushing.

'You sound to me like a girl in love,' he said tightly. 'In which case, of course, it would be absurd for me to try to persuade you to give him up. Your own pride, your own self-respect, apparently mean nothing in the scales against your feelings for this two-faced, sneaking...'

'Max!' She was shocked by the sudden barbaric cruelty in his voice. His usual air of lazy sophistication was totally gone, leaving naked rage behind.

They had reached the great double doors leading into the supper-room. Max dropped his arm from her waist and gave her a stiff little bow.

'Thank you for the dance.' He turned, abandoning her there, his face a mask.

Katrine walked through into the supper-room and found a seat in a quiet corner. Her head ached and she was utterly miserable. She wished she had never come here tonight.

The supper-room had been restored to its former beauty, all the elegance and splendour of its early years in Regency England. The walls were painted the very palest shade of green, with contrasting dark green piping on the panels and woodwork. The chandeliers were glittering, reflecting the dazzle of the silver and glass below. The velvet curtains hung from brass rods, and the carpet was thick and luxurious. The scent of the baskets of flowers hung heavily on the warm air.

She stared up at the chandeliers gloomily. They were like her family—sparkling, tinkling, luminous and quite artificial. 'We're parasites,' she thought. 'That's all we are.'

Nicky found her there a few moments later and lifted her chin with one hand, peering into her eyes. 'Why so sad and wan, fair lady, prithee, why so sad?'

She laughed. 'A little depressed,' she admitted.

'You aren't giving the party a chance! Come back and dance with me! The night is young and you are beautiful. Why shouldn't we have a ball together?' Nicky seemed almost hectic in his gaiety, and she wondered, studying him, what had brought that desperate brightness into his eyes, that almost grimly determined smile to his very handsome. well-cut features.

They danced together for a while, swirling and laughing around the room, putting on a joint performance calculated to convince any onlooker that they were having a fantastic time.

Rolf was dancing with Dodie, Katrine noticed. Dodie was flushed and smiling, her plain face illumined by an inner beauty that no cosmetic could reproduce. Rolf, too, looked extremely contented. Regarding them, Katrine could not help but think wistfully how perfectly they suited each other, and how much she would like it if they should ever grow even closer. But then there was Max ... Her loyalties were painfully divided. Either Max or her father must lose Dodie, and she could not quite bear the thought of either being unhappy.

They joined the rest of their party to sit out a few dances. Cleo and Max were both reserved, but Dodie and Rolf were giggling over a long-ago incident from their mutual past which something had recalled to them. Katrine laughed as they recounted it, interrupting each other all the time, but neither Cleo nor Max seemed particularly amused.

Nicky glanced coolly at Cleo. 'Dance?' he muttered.

She raised one frigid eyebrow. 'Such a courteous invitation could hardly be refused,' she returned unpleasantly.

Nicky's jaw set. 'Would you care to dance?' He used the phrase icily.

Cleo shrugged, stood up, and Nicky jerked her into his arms with a sort of angry snap. Her cheeks reddened. She said something as they danced off, and Nicky made some sort of retort.

Max stood up and looked down at Katrine. 'Shall we?'

She meekly stood up and let him draw her close. As they began to dance, he said, 'Your cousin is going to get a punch on the jaw if he keeps being rude to Cleo.'

She didn't answer. All her attention was concentrated on the moment, on his lean body close to her, the feel of his hand against her waist, the coolness of his fingers gripping hers. Physical sensations of pleasure swamped her. Had she ever disliked this man? It seemed so long ago. She did not even know when exactly she had ceased to dislike him and fallen in love. She stared at the black smoothness of his shoulder just above her eyes. Love ... that was what this was, this melting emotion filling her.

'I must be boring you to tears,' he said suddenly with abrupt ferocity.

She looked up, startled. 'I'm sorry?'

'So you should be. I've spoken to you several times and you didn't hear a word! What's absorbing you to such an extent?' The grey eyes held hers, probing, dissecting.

'Nothing,' she said hurriedly, aware that she was blushing and angry with herself.

His eyebrow lifted. 'It looks very much like something,' he commented drily. 'When a girl blushes like that it's usually a young man at the back of it all ...'

Katrine looked away, biting her lip. His arm tightened cruelly on her waist and she gave a little gasp. 'You're hurting me!' Then she remembered the last time she had said that, the time when he had given her that merciless kiss, and she trembled.

'I'd like to hurt you,' he said tightly. 'I've never known a girl who could make me feel so angry as you do. You're the most infuriating, naïve, obstinate creature I've ever met!'

'I'm sorry if I make you angry,' she said in a thin little voice. 'I don't mean to.'

'Do you know what you mean?' he demanded. 'I don't believe you do. You act like some blind mole, digging furiously in all directions but having no real idea of where it is ...'

I'm in love with you, she thought—that's where I am, and I wish I knew a way of getting out of this unbearable situation, because I know very well there's no possibility of any future for me, no shred of a chance that you would ever look at me. You seem to swing between Cleo and Dodie. Why don't you make up your mind, damn you, Max? Why don't you make up your mind?

Rolf and Dodie were leaving. Rolf never permitted himself a late night when he was in rehearsal. Despite popular fallacies, an actor works very hard at his job, and Rolf worked harder than most. Katrine and Max joined the others at the door, where the Mayor and his wife were shaking hands and being very pleasant. The Mayor gave Max a friendly smile, making some comment about Max's work, then turned to Katrine.

'And this is the lovely little newcomer! Well, Cantwich is certainly going to be proud that you first trod the boards here ... that's the phrase, isn't it? Trod the boards!' He looked very pleased with himself as he repeated it.

She smiled politely. 'Thank you.'

Max gripped her elbow and steered her out. She looked back over her shoulder. Roddy was not in sight, but she saw Nicky and Cleo dancing together. They were not talking and both wore set expressions.

'I think I'd better ...' She half turned to go back, but Max had tight hold of her arm.

'You're going home to bed, young woman,' he snapped.

'I ought to say goodnight to Roddy,' she protested. 'I came with him, but I've hardly set eyes on him ...'

'Good thing too,' said Dodie, overhearing. 'You can drive back with us, darling.'

'I'll take her,' Max said curtly.

Dodie protested, 'You ought to wait for Cleo, Max! Where is she?'

'Nicky will bring her home,' Max said. 'I'll bring this young madam.'

Rolf laughed and steered Dodie away without further argument. Katrine moved to follow them, but Max caught her shoulder and held her back in the dark car park.

'Use your common sense, girl. They don't want any third party tonight.'

Katrine looked up at him, too startled for speech. In the darkness his eyes glittered with a steely light. Was he hurt, angry, jealous? She had wondered if he had noticed how well Dodie and Rolf seemed to look together. Obviously he had. But what was behind this cool attitude of his? Did he merely accept it as inevitable? Did he really feel calm indifference? Or was he more moved than he was permitting to show?

'You ... don't mind?' She meant to phrase the question more tactfully, but distress made her blurt it out.

He looked at her broodingly. 'Do you?'

'Me?' She was surprised into laughing. 'Mind? I'm absolutely delighted. You know how I love Dodie.'

He nodded. 'Dodie was a little concerned, all the same—even the best of relationships can go sour if there's any jealousy, and she knows how you adore your father.'

'I love them both about equally, I would say,' Katrine said honestly. 'Dodie has always been like a mother to me. I couldn't be happier if this comes off ...'

'And the others? Cleo? Viola? Cass? What do you think they will say? Will they object to Rolf marrying Dodie? I've noticed a certain lack of warmth in Cleo towards her lately.'

Katrine looked up at him warily, her lashes flickering. 'Cleo? Well, perhaps she was jealous of someone else ...'

He frowned. 'How do you mean?'

Hesitantly, Katrine said, 'You've been seeing rather a lot of Dodie lately. Cleo may have thought that you were in love with Dodie ...'

They had reached Max's car. He opened the door and helped her in with a hand beneath her elbow. Then he walked round and climbed into the driver's seat. He switched on the internal light and faced her, an arm along the back of the seat.

He looked oddly leashed, as if he were keeping himself on a tight rein. 'So Cleo thought I was in love with Dodie?' He watched her small, pale face. 'Did you, by the way?'

'I thought it seemed likely,' she admitted uneasily.

A hard glint came into the grey eyes. 'What did you think of that? Happy to think of darling Dodie marrying me?' His tones were horridly sarcastic, and she shrank away from him.

'I want whatever will make Dodie happy,' she said huskily.

'Even marriage to me?' He sounded angry, oddly enough. She couldn't think why, except that this discussion must be hurting him somehow or he wouldn't look like that, so grim and controlled.

'Obviously I have no right to choose for her,' she stammered. 'But I'm afraid I would rather she married my father.' She gave him an appealing look, her eyes wide. 'I'm sorry, Max, but Rolf needs her more than you do.'

'You think you know what I need, little girl?' His anger was out in the open now, blazing in the tight nostrils, thinned lips and narrowed eyes.

'You aren't the sort of man to need a woman in that way,' she said nervously.

'In what way?' he pressed sardonically.

She flushed. 'You're too strong, too much of a loner, to need a woman like Dodie to lean on ... in many ways Rolf is weaker than you. He needs love and support.'

'What am I? Some sort of subhuman in no need of love?' He sneered at her. 'What do you know about needs, Katya? You're still a child. There are some needs only a woman can fulfil, but you're too ignorant to know about those, and I pity the man who has to teach you, because you're too much of a coward to be able to give him the response he'll demand.'

Katrine had no answer to give to that. It was not true, but she could hardly assure him of that without betraying herself.

Max drove her home in a deadly silence. She muttered a hurried goodnight in the kitchen and dived upstairs. There was no sign of Rolf and Dodie. She undressed, showered and stood in the darkness of her room staring out into the garden.

A glowing tip of light betrayed Max's presence down there. As if he sensed her above him he turned and glanced up. 'Go to sleep,' his cool voice commanded impartially.

She stayed there briefly, looking down upon the pale oval of his upturned face. She would have liked to have gone down into the scented, breathing darkness and walked with him among the lawns and flowers, listening to the whisper of the trees overhead.

'Goodnight,' she whispered, however, and reluctantly went to bed.

She heard him drop his cigarette, stamp on it and walk away. The garden seemed achingly empty after that. It was a long time before she fell asleep.

CHAPTER NINE

AT breakfast next morning she was astonished to find Rolf and Dodie already seated at the table. Sebby was standing behind them, grinning like an ape. On the table stood a silver wine cooler from which projected a bottle of champagne.

Katrine paused, taking all this in with a rapid glance. Rolf and Dodie gave her a half laughing, half scared smile.

'Is it true?' She ran, ecstatically, to hug them both. 'I can tell by your faces ... oh, it's wonderful! I'm so happy! Dodie, dearest Fra! I did hope it would come true and it has!'

'I told you, Madame,' Sebby said smugly.

'You did,' Dodie nodded to him. She held Katrine close, her smooth cheek pressed against the girl's. 'Darling Katya, thank you for saying all that! Max thought you would be pleased, but I was not sure. I knew you were fond of me, but I was not sure how you would feel about a step-mother ...'

'You've been my second mother for so long that it will just be a sort of legal confirmation of the fact,' Katrine told her. She smiled at her father. 'Lucky Fra! You couldn't have done anything to make me happier.'

Rolf beamed, handsome and golden-bearded in the morning sunlight. 'I'm ashamed to admit that my motives were purely selfish,' he teased her. 'I proposed to her because I want her for my wife. It only later occurred to me that you might like having her as a mother.'

She laughed. 'Wicked Fra! I know you are going to be happy together. I thought last night what a wonderful couple you make. Made for each other.'

Cleo drifted in, wearing an aquamarine silk nightgown rather loosely and inadequately covered by a matching negligee. She stopped, staring at the champagne in puzzled surprise. Then she saw their faces, sheepish, happy, a little eager.

Cleo gave a hard laugh. 'Do I detect a happy event in the offing?'

Dodie did not move to embrace her, as she had with Katrine. Rolf held out his hands to Cleo as he told her simply his news. Cleo looked at him, then at Dodie.

'Congratulations, Dodie. You pulled it off! But what about Max? Isn't he going to object slightly to this jolly event?'

Dodie looked sadly at her. Rolf exclaimed angrily. 'Don't speak to Dodie like that, Cleo! You foul-mouthed, ill-tempered little vixen!'

Cleo sneered back. 'I'm sorry—I can't pretend to be ecstatic over your betrothal scene. Frankly, I find it in poor taste. Aren't you a little old for romance, Fra?'

Rolf went scarlet with rage. He spluttered furiously like a damp squib. Cleo laughed and drifted out before he had time to say all the violently angry things he had boiling in his head.

Dodie restrained him ruefully. 'Forget what she said, darling. I'm afraid poor Cleo is not happy. She has not been happy for a long time.'

'Not since she split with her cousin,' Sebby said very softly.

Katrine spun to stare at him. 'What did you say? Split with whom? Do you mean Nicky?'

Sebby looked back at her stolidly. Rolf sighed. 'There was something between Cleo and Nicky a while back. About two years ago, I think. They were in a production together—a Feydeau farce at the New Horizon. Then suddenly they had a row. Cleo has been difficult ever since.'

'Two years ago?' Katrine had a sudden inspiration. 'I wonder if that was around the time Delia Brett married her dog biscuit king?'

'What?' They all stared at her in dumbfounded amazement.

'Are you all right, darling?' asked Dodie anxiously.

'Perfectly,' Katrine nodded. 'Where's Max?'

'Still in bed,' Sebby grunted. 'Not like him. I think he was late home last night.'

Katrine made for the door without another word. She dived up the stairs and tapped on Max's door. There was no answer. Had he got up already and gone out? She pulled the door open and peered inside hesitantly.

The curtains were drawn tightly. The room lay in shadowed coolness. She tiptoed to the bed and looked down upon his face in repose. The long, bony nose; the firm mouth and jaw, the heavy-lidded eyes—all relaxed in sleep, leaving an impression of surprising youth. His dark hair spilled over the pillow. Tenderly she brushed it back from his forehead.

Quick as a flash his hand shot up and grasped her wrist. She gave a cry of alarm. His eyes were wide open, staring up at her.

'Well, well, well,' he drawled. 'To what do I owe this honour, my girl?'

'Y ... you overslept,' she stammered. 'Rehearsals, remember?' She tugged at her hand, but he would not release it.

'That isn't why you ventured in here,' he said, watching her face thoughtfully. 'Tell me the real reason.'

'You remember you said Roddy published a story about Nicky and a girl called Delia?' She burst out hastily.

'Yes,' he said, watchful.

'Was that two years ago?'

'It might have been,' he admitted.

'Was Nicky dating Cleo then?' she asked point blank.

His brows rose. 'I see. This explains your urgent need to see me. What if he was? Jealous?'

She brushed the question aside. 'Why didn't you tell me? Why didn't Cleo say something? Last summer in Provence ... I felt there was something, but everyone was so tight-lipped about it. Why all the secrecy?'

'You weren't involved. It had nothing to do with you. I doubt if Cleo wanted to broadcast the fact, and Nicky wanted to keep it all as quiet as possible. Delia was sick enough about it as it was, you see. There was a general agreement to keep it quiet.'

'So when Roddy broke that story, he ruined whatever there was between Cleo and Nicky as well as almost stopping Delia's marriage?'

Max nodded. 'Sweet of him, wasn't it?'

'I wonder why he did it.' she murmured, her brow wrinkled in thought.

'Because he's a poisonous little insect,' Max suggested.

She looked down at him, then tugged her hand free. He permitted her to go, but his eyes mocked her as she moved away from the bed.

'Better run, sweetie! I'm getting up now.'

She flushed and escaped without another word. By the time she had finished her breakfast, which included a glass of Fra's best champagne by way of celebration, Dodie and Rolf had driven off together. Cleo, sleekly casual in jeans and a very low-cut silky sweater, was fastidiously finishing her yoghurt while Sebby cleared away the champagne bucket.

Max arrived in time to hear Nicky hooting vociferously at the gate. 'What does he want?' he demanded.

Cleo shrugged. 'Not me,' she said tightly.

Katrine grabbed her copy of the play and ran down the drive. Nicky swung his car door open. 'I want words,' he said.

She climbed in, and they shot off at breakneck speed.

Nicky drove staring straight ahead. After a while, he said, 'Katie, remember last summer?'

'In Provence? Of course,' she said softly.

He shot her a queer look. 'How well?'

She was bewildered. 'Well enough, I suppose. We had a great time. The weather was superb and we had fun.'

'Fun?' He seized on the word eagerly. 'That was all—for you? Just fun? Nothing more?'

She hesitated, then said firmly, 'Nothing more, Nicky. And I don't think it was anything more than fun for you, either, now was it, honestly?'

He let out a long sigh of relief. 'Well, no, frankly. You're a dear, sweet girl, darling, and I played a rotten trick on you. I wanted to make someone jealous, so I flirted with you a lot. I didn't think what effect it might have on you until it was ... pointed out to me last night.'

'Cleo?' she guessed tolerantly. She watched Nicky's very handsome, faintly unstable profile.

'How did you know?'

'It wasn't difficult to guess. What did Cleo say?'

He slowed down and eventually drew in to a grass-edged lay-by where they could talk safely. Turning, he faced her, his arm along the seat. 'Cleo was furious with me about you. She thinks I'm a flirt, completely untrustworthy. She said I'd made you unhappy by playing around with you last summer. I was sure you hadn't taken me seriously, but she wouldn't accept that.'

In fact, she thought wryly, Cleo had not been far wrong. Until recently she had been very unhappy over Nicky. It was only the advent of Max that had cured her. Nicky was a dangerous person to have around if one was an impressionable young girl, like introducing a match into a gunpowder factory. His blond good looks and that facile charm could be devastating.

Aloud, she said, 'I'll speak to Cleo, if you would like me to, Nicky.'

He looked eagerly at her. 'Would you? Tell her what you just told me—that it was all fun for you, too. That should convince her, shouldn't it?'

'Let's hope so,' she agreed. She waited a moment, then said, 'Nicky, tell me something. Why did Roddy publish that story about Delia and you? Did you ever find out?'

'Sheer malice,' Nicky said flatly.

'Oh, I can't believe that,' she protested. She just could not accept that Roddy was so beastly.

Nicky shrugged. 'Why else? Cleo had not known about Delia. You know how proud your sister is— when she read that foul little paragraph about me and Delia she went mad. She refused to see me again, to go out with me. We worked together for months and she never spoke a civil word. I used to have to kiss her twice a night and four times with the matinee. It was sheer bloody hell. It got so bad that I used to break out in a sweat the moment we walked on stage. I shook like a leaf when I was about to kiss her. And Cleo used to look me straight in the face, as cool as a damned cucumber.'

Katrine could imagine Cleo only too well. She had always been a very reserved girl, proud and independent. She would close up in her pain and refuse to allow anyone to suspect her real feelings.

'Poor Cleo,' she said gently.

'Poor Cleo?' Nicky looked affronted. 'Poor me, you mean. You can't imagine what it was like, kissing that stiff-backed little iceberg. She used to give me contemptuous smiles which froze my marrow. I was glad when that run ended. I was at the end of my tether.'

'And I never suspected,' she murmured. 'I must have been blind not to have noticed.'

'I hope I can still act,' Nicky said indignantly. He added drily, 'Cleo isn't bad, either.'

'She's superb,' Katrine said honestly. 'She really fooled me all the time. I thought she hated you.'

Nicky looked gloomy. 'She does. That wasn't acting.'

Katrine eyed him sympathetically. 'I'm not so sure. Last night even I began to notice something between you ...'

'Yes, hate,' he said.

'No,' she shook her head. 'I'll see Cleo. I'm sure you're being too pessimistic.'

Rehearsals started late and progressed badly. Max was in a crisp, no-nonsense mood which involved a number of annihilating remarks scattered indiscriminatingly among the cast. Katrine was not safe from them. Nor was Cleo, who looked blackly at Max without replying. Nicky was a victim once and mistakenly tried to argue only to be slapped down with ruthless toughness by one of Max's unanswerable sallies.

'Who does he think he is? Attila the Hun,' whispered Nicky to Katrine.

Max glared at him. 'If you've got something to say, let us all hear it.'

Nicky mumbled, going dark red. Cleo sneered at him across the stage. The company studied their feet and were politely silent.

The day wore on tediously. Everyone was very careful to keep out of the searchlight of Max's grim gaze. Even Cleo was subdued. When they broke for the day, Katrine caught up with her sister and said, 'I want to talk to you. Come for a cup of tea?'

'Max is driving me home,' Cleo drawled.

'Please,' Katrine said.

Cleo stared at her, shrugged. 'Oh, very well. I'll ask Max to wait, but I can't think why it can't wait until we're home.' She caught Max as he walked off, and said, 'Can you hang on for half an hour? Katrine wants a private chat with me.'

Max turned his dark gaze upon Katrine. His face was impenetrable. 'Very well. I'll be in the office.'

They got a cup of tea at the restaurant and took it out on to the terrace by the river. The water had a shimmering haze hanging over its surface, reflecting the deep blue of the summer sky, so that it looked like a willow-edged piece of broken mirror on which floated the usual flotilla of ducks.

'From troubles of the world I turn to ducks,' quoted Cleo lightly. She stirred her tea. 'Well?'

Katrine huskily cleared her throat and began. 'I just wanted to tell you I'm not in love with Nicky,' she said.

Cleo stiffened, her cheeks suddenly dark red, her eyes furious and fixed on Katrine's face. 'What? Did he ask you to come and tell me that? Why, that ...' She bit off whatever she had been about to say with a white snap of her teeth.

'You told him you thought I was,' Katrine said hurriedly. 'I'm not doing this very well ...'

'No, you're not,' Cleo agreed.

'But you see, you've got it so wrong. I did rather like Nicky once, last summer. It was very romantic in Provence ...'

'Heady stuff,' Cleo drawled cynically. 'A moon over blue waters, a guitar playing in the background, the perfume of many flowers from the perfume factory fields behind the town, the sweet nothings Nicky kept whispering in your shell-like ear ...'

'Yes, you may laugh, but those things have their effect,' said Katrine, blushing.

'You bet they do, as Nicky knows. He's an expert, believe me. He plays potent melodies on that flute-like voice of his.' Cleo was bitter beneath her light tone. 'You fell for him. Don't deny it.'

'I don't deny it. But once I was back in England

things looked different. Lately I've been totally indifferent to him.'

Cleo looked sharply at her. 'Indifferent?'

Katrine nodded earnestly. 'He's more my brother than my boyfriend. I like him, but nothing more than that. Honestly, Cleo, that is all.'

Cleo bit her lower lip. 'Well, fine. Lucky you. Join the band of happy escapees from the well-nigh fatal Nicky Milford charm.'

'Don't!' Katrine hated the sharpness underlying Cleo's light words. It was very revealing.

'Oh, believe me, lots haven't got away in time. The deserts of theatre land are littered with their bleaching bones!'

'Nicky cares about you, Cleo,' Katrine said.

Cleo turned on her, standing up in a graceful, angry movement. 'I didn't come out here to hear you repeating phoney messages from that double-crossing little creep! If Nicky had any guts he would not send you of all people to me.'

Katrine watched her walk back towards the car park, her red-gold hair glinting like coins in the sunlight. She rose and languidly followed her, dropping her paper cup into the litter bin as she passed.

Max and Cleo were in the car when she arrived. Max got out and opened the back seat door, gesturing to her to get in. 'Everyone else has gone,' he told her curtly.

Cleo was silent for the whole of the drive. Her hair blew softly across Max's shoulder. Once or twice he casually put up a hand to brush away a silken strand from his neck. The intimacy of the gesture wounded Katrine more than she could admit.

That evening they all stayed home to celebrate Rolf and Dodie's engagement. No news of it had crept out in the press as yet, and they were hoping to keep it out of the papers for a while.

'No word to Roddy Sumner,' warned Max, at his most dictatorial. Katrine nodded without verbal response since she was so irritated by his autocratic manner that she would have loved to slap him and knock the patronising sneer from his face.

'Katrine has grown up with discretion,' Dodie said in her defence.

Max smiled lazily. 'You astonish me! Who would have thought it from the way she behaves!'

Dodie eyed him oddly. 'Max, Max,' she murmured in a very gentle voice, and Max, equally oddly, went dark red and left the room.

Rehearsals next day were far more successful. The company was becoming a unit, acting more smoothly together, finding the tempo Max had been trying to reach.

Max was apparently as untouched by success as he had been by catastrophe. He was the same tyrannical, unbending task master who was determined to wrench a performance out of them if he could not get one by kindness.

As the days went on it became plain that Max was manipulating them. He would show them a bland face, talk and smile with warmth as the rehearsal went on—only to change suddenly and shout, crack the whip, lash them with sarcasm and contempt. Then the storm would blow away and the fair weather would set in once more.

He used varying techniques to mould them, altering completely if he felt he was not reaching a certain actor. Some of them would only work when driven. Others needed sympathy and constant understanding. One or two of the female members of the cast worked best when he flirted with them—to them a sexual persuasion was all important. Max was all things to all of them. He seemed to sense which approach was best in each situation, and adjust accordingly.

Watching him work, Katrine was overcome with admiration for him.

With her, he still used largely persuasion, except when he lost his temper, and that was rarely over her work.

She always felt very clumsy, very large and awkward, at the start of rehearsals. Her feet seemed to trip her up. Her hands felt like sausages. She would stumble on stage, flushed and shaking, a sick sensation in the pit of her stomach.

But once rehearsals were under way she lost all this fear. She became immersed in the character she was playing. Her body grew so light she barely felt it. Her own emotions, fears, dreams fell away and she took on this other personality; a shy, eager, terrified young girl lost in nightmare, crying silently for help with eloquent gestures.

The dress rehearsal culminated for her in her final scene—her one speech. When she did speak at last she felt all her grief and despair ringing out, reaching out to the audience. It was a moment which left her exhausted, wrung.

As the curtain fell, Dodie turned to her and embraced her with a weeping sincerity which was more of an accolade than the loudest applause. Katrine knew that she, herself, was crying because there were tears running into her mouth at the corners, but she was so totally absorbed in the moment that she was unable to feel anything.

The rest of the company crowded round her, congratulating her. Then Max was on stage, as taut as a whip lash, his face pale and set.

'What the hell is this? A mutual admiration society? We haven't had the inquest yet, so don't start thinking you can all relax and go home. I've got a list of problems as long as the Forth Bridge. So you can stop patting each other on the back and hear the truth about that abortion of a performance...'

They all stared at him, taken aback and downcast. He gestured to them to sit down. Then he took them apart, one by one, bitterly cross-questioning them, pointing out failures and praising where they had succeeded. They listened intently, frowning.

It was a long time before they were allowed to go home, and by then their momentary euphoria had quite evaporated.

Katrine looked at Dodie, angry and hurt. 'Why

was he so completely merciless? It wasn't that bad!'

Dodie smiled at her reassuringly. 'It is bad luck to make too much of a dress rehearsal. Often that makes the cast relax, then they are lazy and bad on the first night. A bad dress rehearsal makes for a good first night.'

'I see,' said Katrine, not quite sure that she did see. Cleo laughed, which was surprising, since Max had been particularly hard on her.

'Darling, even if we have a smash hit of a first night, Max will be at our throats next morning with another little list of weak points for us to work on ... don't imagine for a moment that rehearsals stop just beause we've gone into production! Max will keep us on our toes.'

Nicky joined them, eyeing Cleo uncertainly. She gave him a long, cold stare in return. Katrine discreetly moved off with Dodie to join Rolf and Max.

Max glanced across at Nicky and Cleo. Then he looked at Katrine, raising those pointed eyebrows. 'Know all about it now, do you? Perhaps you can see why I told you that your cousin was worthless.'

'Nicky isn't worthless. He has been unlucky,' she said with hot loyalty. 'But he really loves Cleo ...' Then, realising that she was speaking to Max who, also, perhaps loved Cleo, she went pale and compressed her lips.

'Is that what he told you?' Max questioned her, his tone acid. 'You really can fool some of the people all of the time, can't you?'

'Nicky meant it. He loves Cleo, I'm sure of it.'

Max's grey eyes probed her face. He sounded bitter, angry, disillusioned. 'What did he hand you? A consolation prize? A few goodbye kisses? Or have you decided it was Roddy you preferred anyway? You certainly know how to pick second-rate men. It must be a unique gift.'

She found his tone so unpleasant that she glared at him with wounded dislike. She was strung up, emotionally drained, after the dress rehearsal. One of these painful squabbles with Max was the last thing she needed.

She followed Dodie and Rolf out to the car and drove off with them, eager to be home and free to relax.

When she got back she had a shower and went to bed, her appetite completely vanished. Sebby did not argue. He knew it was best to let nature take its course.

She slept badly, waking from time to time with a feeling of intense fear, a suffocating terror which she could not shake off.

At last the darkness faded and pale light crept across the room to the sound of the morning chorus from the birds. She dressed and went down to the kitchen. Sebby was already down, squeezing oranges. He looked at her, gestured to the coffee pot. She sighed. 'How do I look?'

'Terrible,' he said frankly. 'Like an old grey blanket.'

She giggled. 'I wish there was some way out of this,' she said after another moment. 'I wish I'd never agreed to do it. I've got a feeling that it is going to be the most disastrous evening of my whole life!'

CHAPTER TEN

MAX insisted that Katrine rest for several hours that afternoon. She protested that she felt perfectly fit, but he firmly led her up to her room, drew the curtains to shut out the sunlight and turned down the covers on her bed.

'You may not be able to sleep, but you must try to relax,' he insisted. 'The others are accustomed to this, don't forget. You're new to it. It will be tiring, at first. This is a long play—two and three-quarter hours on stage, and you're out there for almost the whole of that time, even if you're not saying anything. Just standing or sitting on that stage will be an enormous emotional strain. Lie down. Keep still. Try not to think about anything.'

When he had gone Katrine took off her dress, slipped into her cotton dressing-gown and lay down obediently. The shady room was full of drowsy summer sounds. Birds twittered in the trees outside. Somewhere a man was mowing a lawn. A breeze rustled through her curtains, blowing them to and fro, making shifting patterns of light on the bedroom walls.

She lay watching them. She tried not to think about the performance. She tried to make her mind empty, but unbidden ideas crowded to force themselves upon her. She started to worry about failure again, and at once perspiration sprang out on her forehead. She struggled vainly against a recurring picture of herself being booed off stage, or somehow worse, being watched in stony silence by a large, hostile audience.

Why was she doing this? Why expose herself to shame and public humiliation? She twisted on the bed, biting her lip. At last she sat up violently. Max's idea had been disastrous. Far from feeling rested. she was feeling hunted. It would have been better if she had spent the afternoon in the kitchen with Sebby. making cakes or whisking eggs for mayonnaise.

She went to the bathroom and took a cool shower, dressed again and went downstairs.

Max was in the garden, reading in a deckchair. He looked at her with a frown as she came towards him. 'Why are you down here? I thought I told you to rest?'

'I couldn't,' Katrine said tersely.

His grey eyes searched her face. 'All right,' he said. 'Come and play chess with me. It will occupy your mind.'

'I'm going to bake a cake,' she said. 'I find that very relaxing.'

Max looked doubtful for a moment, then he suddenly smiled, his face full of that individual charm she was unable to resist. 'Each to his own,' he conceded. 'Make it a chocolate cake. I love them. With mint-flavoured icing—like the one you made when you first arrived down here.'

Sebby was drinking tea with his feet resting on a chair. He grinned at her. 'Fed up with resting? I wondered how long you would stick it. Get yourself a cup.'

Katrine poured herself some tea, then began to gather together the ingredients for Max's chocolate-mint cake. Soon she was quite absorbed, her mind at ease now that her body was active. There was something so comforting about these automatic actions. While she was doing mundane tasks she could set her mind free. Her fears and worries seemed less looming. She felt more able to meet any problems. Her confidence blossomed once more.

For a few hours she was happier, but as the time wore on she grew more and more nervous. As they drove in to the theatre she was quite openly trembling, her cold hands pressed together in her lap, her face as white as the lace collar on her dress.

Backstage it was crowded. The noise was deafening to her. Excited, anxious, over exuberant young people swirled to and fro. Last minute wardrobe alterations were being made. The stage hands were in busy conference over a door which kept sticking. A paint-splattered designer was frowning ferociously over copies of the second act backcloth, trying to think of a way of toning it down since Max had decided it was too intrusive, too obvious.

Katrine dressed with shaking hands. Seated in front of her mirror, she opened telegrams, read them with blurred eyesight, making little of their good wishes. Viola and Cass came back to kiss her and wish her luck.

Viola was cheerfully looking forward to her wedding day. 'I seem to be coping quite well with housekeeping, don't I, Cass?'

Cass grinned. 'You haven't poisoned me yet. Geoffrey seems prepared to accept whatever you offer him, so I should say you're safe enough.'

They were delighted to have Katrine inside the professional fold. 'Now all the Milfords are in the business!' Cass kissed her warmly. 'One day *we* must do something together.' He grinned at his father, who had just come into the dressing-room. 'Why should Fra have all the fun?'

'Quite right,' said Rolf cheerfully. 'All the luck, darling.' He kissed her, his beard tickling her cheek. 'We're going to have a great time in this play.'

Cleo put her head round the door, nodded to Viola and Cass. 'What's this? Family gathering? I just popped in to wish Katie luck. You, too, Fra.'

Max interrupted them with a stern face. 'Sorry to break up this idyllic family scene, but I want Katrine to have a short rest before she has to go on ... so hop it, the rest of you. Don't forget, she's new to all this.'

Then she and Max were alone. She sat down again, a sigh almost torn out of her.

'Nervous?' he asked, his penetrating gaze fixed on her face in the mirror.

'Petrified,' she admitted.

He nodded. 'Naturally. We all are on first nights. Some are sick. Some are stiff as pokers. But we're all affected.'

'Viola always felt sick, she said.'

'It will pass once you're on,' he assured her.

Katrine smiled. 'Yes.' She was white under her make-up, her blue eyes enormous.

He knelt and took her hands between his own, exclaiming angrily as he felt how cold and stiff they were. 'My God, you're like ice!' He rubbed her fingers, his head bent.

She looked down at him and felt a sickening flood of love welling up within her. With the heavy-lidded eyes veiled like that, their cynical intelligence hidden, his features took on a strange brooding tenderness.

'I hope I don't let you down,' she said huskily.

He raised his head. There was surprise and something else in his eyes. He still held her hands, his fingers cool. 'I have no doubts on that score,' he said gently. 'Neither need you have, my dear. You won't fail.'

She laughed nervously. 'I hope you're right.'

'I'm always right,' he said, as he had said before. 'You may not trust yourself, Katya, but I wish you could learn to trust me.' His voice was gently chiding.

She smiled. 'I do trust you.' Then her real feelings

broke through the polite assurance, and her voice deepened with emotion as she added, 'I'd trust you with anything.'

He looked as if he might say something, and her heart began to thud as she caught a gleam of something odd in those grey eyes. Then he suddenly drew back, stood up, relinquishing her hands.

'I'll leave you to relax before you go on,' he said abruptly. 'Just trust me and forget everything else.' He paused, hesitatingly, looking down at her.

Katrine waited, sensing that he was going to kiss her, as the others had done.

The kiss was light, neutral, very gentle. It left her aching and disappointed, yet somehow relieved. Had Max kissed her in any other way, she knew perfectly well, she would have been far too strung up to relax.

It seemed only a moment after he had left her that she was standing in the wings waiting for her cue. Then came the dazzle of lights, the outer waiting, breathing darkness and the feeling of unbounded panic as she thought of all those eyes out there watching her, like the eyes of animals in the jungle, waiting for the moment when they would pounce for the kill.

For a brief while she was torn between this fear and her sense of what she should be doing, then gradually she fell into the pattern of movement she had established. She forgot the audience, except with one detached part of her mind. She lived within the mind of another girl, suffering with her, feeling with her, thinking with her.

She moved within the context of the play, her thin body taking on a gawkiness, a clumsiness which was extremely moving. In her white face her eyes stared despairingly. She was pathetic in her youth, her need, her hopelessness.

When she reached the final part of the play, and burst into her brief, heart-rending speech, she felt, suddenly, the silence of the house, the eyes fixed on her. They were utterly attentive, involved with what she was saying. She held them, and it charged her speech with an extra dimension of power.

When she ended there was a silence for so long that she began to shake.

Then the lights dimmed. And the applause began. It crashed on and on, like waves beating on a rocky shore, and Katrine felt dazed by it, bewildered as though she were trapped by the sound and could not escape.

Somehow she responded with the rest of the company. They bowed, linked hands, bowed again. Rolf and Dodie came forward, hand in hand. The applause rose in volume. Then Cleo was invited forward by her father and also received an enthusiastic welcome. Then, to Katrine's stunned bewilderment and disbelief, the three main players turned and gestured to her to come down to the footlights. She was rooted to the spot, trembling.

Dodie swept towards her, took her hand and gently led her under a deafening barrage of applause. The audience stamped, whistled and cheered. Katrine did not even know that she was crying until Dodie, leading her off into the wings, dabbed at her wet cheeks with a handkerchief and said, 'Oh, my dear, my dearest ...' in loving, scolding tenderness.

Cleo said, half laughing, 'I rather think a star is born, if that isn't too ludicrously trite ... Katie, you've wasted years of your life, but you've made it at last, thanks to Max.'

Wet-faced and trembling still, Katrine looked around for Max, but he was not in sight, and her heart plummeted. She longed to thank him, to see him. Just to see him would ease her longings.

Then, suddenly, among the pushing throng of people shaking hands, hugging and talking, she saw him.

He was in shirt sleeves, his air abstracted, a frown on his face. At his side was the ASM, talking fast. Even now Max was working, even while the excited audience streamed out of the theatre into the summer night.

Cleo pushed through the crowd and flung herself into Max's arms, her hands clasping his face. 'Angel! Thank you. We owe it all to you ...'

Max looked tolerant, bent his head and kissed her on the mouth, his hands linking at her waist.

A knife plunged into Katrine's heart and twisted viciously. She swallowed, turning away.

It was difficult to fight her way through to her dressing-room through the people wishing to talk to her, congratulate her, say words of praise. She smiled, thanked them and felt sick.

Dodie and Fra kissed her. Viola and Cass, Cleo again, then Nicky. Katrine wondered if this was really happening to her. Until tonight she had been on the outside, looking in; she had watched this madhouse from a distance, she had gone backstage to wish her family luck, then to congratulate them after a triumphant first night. Now it was happening to her, and she hated it.

Faces, voices, hands touching, eyes staring ... she was sure she was going mad.

Then something happened. A blankness. She went whiter and whiter, slowly she crumpled to the floor.

'Katya!' Dodie cried in dismay, kneeling beside the small, still body.

'What's wrong?' demanded voice after voice. Rolf was alarmed, demanding, 'Is she sick?'

Max pushed his way, shouldering people aside ruthlessly, and bent to lift her in his arms. He carried her into her dressing-room and slammed the door shut.

Dodie opened it. Behind her the faces pressed. Max turned on them all a grim, unsmiling face.

'Out! Everybody!'

Dodie took one look at him and was gone. The door closed and it was quiet in the tiny stuffy room.

Katrine slowly opened her eyes, feeling the awful pressure lift from her. Max was beside her, kneeling at the couch, his grey eyes fixed on her face.

Roughly, he asked, 'How do you feel now?'

'I'm sorry,' she whispered. 'It was too much ...'

'The performance?' he asked tersely.

She shook her head. 'No, afterwards ... so many people ...' She did not add that she had only really felt the terrible pressure building up at the back of her head when she saw him kiss her sister.

He looked at her angrily. 'You should have gone straight to your dressing-room, not let them prey on you like that ... in future, I'll make damned sure it's clear backstage. I hate a cluttered back house ...'

She lay back, closing her eyes. He took a piece of cotton wool, soaked it in cologne and gently wiped her forehead, and then the rest of her face. His fingers stroked soothingly over her skin. She did not want him to stop. The movement was so deliciously comforting.

Quietly, he said, 'I suppose you're wondering why I haven't added my praise to all that adulation you had out there?'

Katrine lay very still. 'No,' she said, her lips only just moving to say the word.

'You little liar,' he said mockingly.

Her lids fluttered upward. She peeped at him, crossly. He was looking at her with a twist of his lips, his eyes full of tolerant amusement.

'I haven't said anything because for once I'm lost for words. You gave me everything I had asked for, and then more. I knew you were going to be good. I was wrong. I think you're possibly going to be a great actress.' He spoke in a low, sombre tone, as if what he said was painful to say, yet the eyes watching her still held that old mockery.

She flushed with pleasure and incredulity. 'Max...'

He laughed abruptly. 'Well? Is that all you're going to say?' The mockery deepened. 'Cleo kissed me...'

She hesitated, then flung caution to the winds and raised herself, her hands shyly touching his shoulders. He watched her as she bent foward to kiss him. He looked cool, wary, unreadable. She had no way of guessing what he was thinking.

Her kiss was light, shy, brief. When she drew back, Max gave her another little smile. 'Thank you. Not quite in the same class as Cleo's, but no doubt you'll improve in that direction, too. She's far more experienced.'

She was cut to the quick by this comparison. 'I'm sorry if I disappointed you.'

He looked patronising. 'You can't help it, child. You're still emotionally frozen.'

Her cheeks flushed hotly. 'I'm nothing of the kind!'

'Prove it,' he challenged, his eyes daring her.

Katrine had reacted to this provocation before she knew what she was doing. With blazing eyes and scarlet cheeks, she flung herself at him, as Cleo had done earlier, and kissed him with the unleashed passion which had been building up inside her for weeks. Her arms wound round his neck, her body clung to his, she sunk herself in a moment of sheer madness.

Then realisation hit her, she drew back, horrified, ashamed. Her huge eyes met his and she winced. 'I ... oh, no ...' She pushed him away, tried to scramble to her feet, writhing in humiliation.

Max could hardly doubt now that she was in love with him. She had made her feelings too horribly plain. How he must be laughing at her! If he was not embarrassed and amused ...

'Katya, my love ...'

The words halted her, incredulously, in her flight.

He sounded incredibly serious. She dared to look at him again. He was pale, his face taut, the grey eyes full of a leaping emotion she had never seen in them before.

He caught her, pulled her close, her head against him, his hands moving over her shoulders and back, his strong fingers stroking, caressing, soothing. She lay against him weakly, sunk in a sensation of bliss.

'I love you,' he said hoarsely. 'You infuriate and annoy me and I'm crazy about you. I don't know what it is about you that sends me off my head—I just know that whenever I see you I feel like kissing you until you beg for mercy. Your bones are so fragile I could break them without any effort, you're shy and nervous and stupidly brave, and Katya, if you don't say you'll marry me I'm going to have to take stern measures.'

She was lost in happy incredulity. Hardly thinking, she touched his hard cheek, the line of his jaw, his mouth.

Max made a strange, strangled noise at the back of his throat, caught her even closer and kissed her with a slow, demanding persistence. She felt as if the warm summer night had completely enveloped them, dragging them down into a sensual darkness which left them quite exhilarated yet blissfully weary.

Later, her head on his shoulder, she listened while he again told her how much he loved her. He was more himself now, the cool and supercilious master of his own fate. Yet at the back of those grey eyes she still saw the shadow of passion, the passion which had so astonished her earlier.

'I can't remember when I first realised I loved you,' he said. 'It grew on me slowly. After that, I saw you more clearly, and I began to suspect you had it in you to make an actress, if only you could be coaxed into having faith in yourself. Dodie agreed with me, and she was able to bring Rolf into the plot. We were all aware that you needed confidence—I don't think Rolf at that stage realised how good you were. He just loved his little daughter. I loved the woman I knew you could be.' He gave her a teasing smile. 'The woman I'm going to make you.'

Katrine flickered a provocative smile up at him. 'What makes you think I'm not that woman now?'

His eyes touched her lips, her throat, moved downwards with a mocking glint. 'Don't tempt me,

Katya. I'm a man under great pressure as it is—I shall have to wait until Viola is married before I can decently get you to church. Two Milford weddings too soon might be more than the world can bear.'

'Why not a double wedding?' she suggested.

Max laughed outright. 'That shows you're still a dear little innocent. What? Viola share her big day? You must be joking. She may be fond of you, but she would turn that idea down very fast.'

She smiled. 'Don't be cynical.'

'I know the Milfords,' he said. 'They perform on a vast stage—the whole world is their audience. They're never off stage, in fact. They perform during every waking minute.'

'Me, too?' she asked in mock annoyance.

'You?' He touched her cheek tenderly. 'You're a changeling, we all know that.'

There was a knock at the door, then Roddy Sumner stuck his head round. His brows jerked together as he saw them, entwined lovingly on the couch.

'Sorry, I seem to be intruding ...' His voice was stiff. 'I just dropped in to offer my congratulations.'

'And now you have a double reason for it,' said Max with great enjoyment. 'Katrine just promised to marry me.'

Roddy stared at her. 'I see. Yes, well, congratulations.' He drew breath. 'Can I use that?'

Max gestured. 'Why not?'

Roddy nodded, turned on his heel and was gone

without another word. Katrine stared at the closed door, puzzled.

'He seemed rather put out.'

Max gave her a shrewd, wry look. 'Didn't he just?'

She looked up at him, wide-eyed. 'What is it, Max? Don't be enigmatic!'

'My dear girl, Roddy Sumner has quite obviously been in love with you for weeks. I think he loved you before I did, but he didn't know it. He must have more intelligence than I gave him credit for—he saw past your shy façade too.'

She was bright pink and horrified. 'You must be wrong! Roddy in love with me? No, Max!'

'Yes, Max,' he mocked. 'Why do you think I detested the fellow? I was very afraid you liked him too—you defended him so fiercely.' He frowned. 'I found out why he published the story about Nicky and Delia, by the way—apparently the dog biscuit king's first wife got on to the old affair between those two, and tried to scotch her ex-husband's new romance by having the story made public. But Delia presumably had more of a hold over the fellow than had been thought, because he still married her.'

'Who told you?' she asked him.

'Roddy himself. I asked him because I was curious—he was pumping me about something else and it killed two birds with one stone. It changed the subject, and it cleared my mind about him.' Max grimaced. 'I'm sorry for the chap. For the first time in his opportunist career I think he genuinely cared for someone other than his miserable self.'

She was unhappy. 'Don't say that! I'm sure Roddy was never in love with me. He used to call me Cinderella and urge me to be more sure of myself ...' Her tone was unwittingly sad, half admitting that she believed Max.

He watched her expressive little face. 'Never mind Roddy Sumner,' he said. 'You must change and come on to the party. I imagine there are hordes of people out there dying to get another look at you.'

She shivered. 'I'm frightened. Max, don't let's go to the party ... Let's stay here together. Once we open that door we let the world in on us. We're safe and peaceful here.'

By that incredible magic which love releases, Max understood. 'I know. This is our secret world and we don't want them in it. But we can't stay here for ever, darling. We have to come out now and then. You have to face up to the fact that you've become famous overnight, one of the Milfords at last, in every sense of the word. You belong to the world as much as you do to me, in some ways. You have to go out there and accept what the world offers you —money, fame, love. We all have to accept what the world gives us.'

'It's terrifying,' she whispered, shivering.

'Yes,' he agreed. 'But it's exciting, too, and whenever the world out there is too much for us, we have our own secret world to retreat to—a world of love and peace into which they cannot follow us.'

She sighed. 'You are a comfort, Max. I'm going to

need you every minute of my life from now on...'

'I'll be there,' he promised. 'And the others will be there, too: Rolf, Dodie, your sisters and Cass. We all love you.'

'If only Cleo would forgive Nicky,' she said. 'Things would be quite perfect.'

'She will,' he soothed. 'Nicky has too much charm and poor old Cleo is too well hooked to escape him. She's struggled valiantly, but she knows Nicky is her fate, just as you're mine, you soft-hearted, pig-headed little angel.'

Katrine wrinkled her nose at him teasingly. 'Charming! I shall never be vain with you to say things like that to me, shall I?'

'If you become vain, I'll beat you,' he promised.

She smiled and then said seriously, 'Although I'm not sure if I want to act any more.'

Max looked dumbfounded. 'Not act any more? My God, what are you saying? After this triumph...'

'Yes, but Max, what about when we start a family?' She was very earnest. 'You're in your thirties. You'll want to have children soon, won't you?' Her eyes grew soft. 'I do, I know. A boy and a girl—just two. I want to look after them myself—no nannies for my children. It will be such fun...'

Max was looking at her incredulously. 'You mean you would give up the theatre again, despite having made such a hit, just to have babies?'

'What do you mean, just to have babies?' She was indignant. 'I love children, and I shall adore our children because they'll be yours, darling. You know how tough life can be for the kids of show business families. There's nothing so important to a child as security and love. I mean to give ours all the love there is ...'

Max lifted her hands to his lips, kissed them almost humbly, with a gesture strange in so arrogant and compelling a man. 'I'm not good enough for you, Katya. Are you sure you can't do better than marry an old cynic like me?'

She laughed at him. 'Silly!' She broke off in a daydream, only to hear Max laughing softly to himself, and looked at him in vague inquiry. 'What is it?'

Max grinned at her, his grey eyes alight with amusement. 'I was just imagining Rolf's face the day he becomes a grandfather. He won't know whether to smile or scowl! It will put a permanent end to his belief that he's still a heart-throb. He'll have to assume the majestic authority of the grandfather figure instead!'

She laughed. 'Oh, poor Fra! How true! How he'll hate that! But he'll put a brave face on it and he'll be a doting grandfather, and Dodie, of course, will be angelic.'

Max grinned. 'One day I'll enlighten Dodie as to your odd belief that I was in love with her. She'll be tickled pink. You do realise she's ten years my senior?'

'She's still beautiful,' said Katrine, laughing and flushed with self-mockery.

Max looked at her with grey eyes alight with passion. 'Not as beautiful as you. No woman could be.'

Someone knocked tentatively on the door and Max grimaced. 'The world is breaking in on us, I'm afraid. Brace yourself, love.'

'Kiss me quickly,' she said. 'I think I could walk through fire if you kissed me first...'

Max did not need to be asked twice. He kissed her, and the knocking on the door did not distract either of them from the brief exchange of passionate, silent vows.

Mills & Boon have commissioned four of your favourite authors to write four tender romances.

Guaranteed love and excitement for St. Valentine's Day

A BRILLIANT DISGUISE	-	Rosalie Ash
FLOATING ON AIR	-	Angela Devine
THE PROPOSAL	-	Betty Neels
VIOLETS ARE BLUE	-	Jennifer Taylor

Available from January 1993   PRICE £3.99

*Available from Boots, Martins, John Menzies, W.H. Smith,
most supermarkets and other paperback stockists.
Also available from Mills & Boon Reader Service, PO Box 236,
Thornton Road, Croydon, Surrey CR9 3RU.*

THE PERFECT GIFT FOR MOTHER'S DAY

Specially selected for you – four tender and heartwarming Romances written by popular authors.

LEGEND OF LOVE -
Melinda Cross

AN IMPERFECT AFFAIR -
Natalie Fox

LOVE IS THE KEY -
Mary Lyons

LOVE LIKE GOLD -
Valerie Parv

Available from February 1993   Price: £6.80

*Available from Boots, Martins, John Menzies, W.H. Smith, most supermarkets and other paperback stockists.
Also available from Mills & Boon Reader Service, PO Box 236, Thornton Road, Croydon, Surrey CR9 3RU.
(UK Postage & Packing free)*

Next Month's Romances

Each month you can choose from a wide variety of romance with Mills & Boon. Below are the new titles to look out for next month, why not ask either Mills & Boon Reader Service or your Newsagent to reserve you a copy of the titles you want to buy — just tick the titles you would like and either post to Reader Service or take it to any Newsagent and ask them to order your books.

Please save me the following titles:	Please tick	√
AN OUTRAGEOUS PROPOSAL	Miranda Lee	
RICH AS SIN	Anne Mather	
ELUSIVE OBSESSION	Carole Mortimer	
AN OLD-FASHIONED GIRL	Betty Neels	
DIAMOND HEART	Susanne McCarthy	
DANCE WITH ME	Sophie Weston	
BY LOVE ALONE	Kathryn Ross	
ELEGANT BARBARIAN	Catherine Spencer	
FOOTPRINTS IN THE SAND	Anne Weale	
FAR HORIZONS	Yvonne Whittal	
HOSTILE INHERITANCE	Rosalie Ash	
THE WATERS OF EDEN	Joanna Neil	
FATEFUL DESIRE	Carol Gregor	
HIS COUSIN'S KEEPER	Miriam Macgregor	
SOMETHING WORTH FIGHTING FOR	Kristy McCallum	
LOVE'S UNEXPECTED TURN	Barbara McMahon	

If you would like to order these books in addition to your regular subscription from Mills & Boon Reader Service please send £1.70 per title to: Mills & Boon Reader Service, P.O. Box 236, Croydon, Surrey, CR9 3RU, quote your Subscriber No:..
(If applicable) and complete the name and address details below. Alternatively, these books are available from many local Newsagents including W.H.Smith, J.Menzies, Martins and other paperback stockists from 12th February 1993.

Name:..
Address:..
....Post Code:........................

To Retailer: If you would like to stock M&B books please contact your regular book/magazine wholesaler for details.

You may be mailed with offers from other reputable companies as a result of this application.
If you would rather not take advantage of these opportunities please tick box ☐